Fantastica – Surreal Prose & Poetry

By Andrea Lightfoot

Table of Contents

INTRODUCTION

Welcome to Fantastica, one of the most phenomenal and mysterious places in the world. The book you are reading contains stories, poems, letters and various articles from this land that is accessible via portals and trapdoors in certain locations in every city all over the world.

Here you will find plenty to see and do, amid breath-taking landscapes; luxurious hotels, gymnasium and leisure centre, museums and stately gardens are just a few of the places of interest here. Reading through this book will give you more information on more of what you can discover while here. It is also worth noting that there is an abundance of shops, restaurants and cafés, and any purchases can be paid for by any currency in the world, or by selling a personal item that you are able to give up. A word of caution here – do not let anyone force you into handing over anything you would not feel comfortable about, i.e. mobile phone or purse.

Home to many people, as well as "magic-wielding" folk, and those of the paranormal variety, seen by those who have this special gift, Fantastica offers the quickest way to Fairyland, for those who wish to visit there. Please be aware however, that a trip to Fairyland means anyone who does not have the use of magic must be accompanied by someone who does.

Fantastica is believed to be as ancient as Fairyland, and some believe it was actually created by magical folk in collaboration with Mother Nature. Together, both Fantastica and Fairyland are one country - the Mystical Realms, although they do have separate councils and governments.

As far as religion is concerned, all different beliefs are followed here, Wicca and Druidism being the main denominations.

For visitors who are interested in yoga, Pilates, meditation or any other form of relaxation, you will certainly find it in Fantastica. A few pieces in this book will (hopefully) inspire you.

We hope that you enjoy your visit here, and that this book gives you not only information on Fantastica and its literature, but a source of inspiration for your daily life.

Vosotha Letio

On behalf of Fantastica High Council

A Letter to Diana

(Written by two sisters, who live in Fantastica, to a close friend, living elsewhere, when they were guests for the first time at one of the most beautiful hotels in Fantastica. They are currently employed there and enjoy the complimentary benefits of working for this five star guesthouse).

Dear Diana,

You should see the room in the Fantasium Hotel that Zophia and I are staying in while we're on holiday. It's absolutely beautiful. You'd love it. It is on the second floor and it is enormous.

The curtains are a deep purple, luxurious velvet and if only you could be here to see the magnificent view! Our room faces the stately gardens where you can see the flowers, trees, maze, gazebo and fountains.

The room is painted black, and white, silver, blue and pink stars glitter in the dark. There are candles which are set into black metal holders that are attached to the wall, and tiny fairy lights which are dotted all over the dark ceiling.

The carpet is the same colour as the curtains and is so soft, you can walk on it barefoot.

The little kitchen has a black and white glittery floor and the cupboards are made of pine wood. There's an oven and also a fireplace. Upon the mantelpiece stand curious knick-knacks.

Then there's our beds! Double beds, with white sheets, and sky blue quilt covers and pillows – apparently they're blue because it is a "relaxing", "tranquil" colour used to help aid sleep.

The bathroom has black and white checked marble tiles and the bath is huge! It is pristine white and has gold taps, one with a ruby on top to show it is the hot tap, the other with a sapphire to indicate it as the cold tap. There is also a "dream-shower" cubicle. We're bringing home a complimentary set of "Fairy-Dust Natural Bath Bubbles, shower gel and shampoo. They smell heavenly. There's also a Jacuzzi.

We're both going out for tea with Mum and Dad, then we're going salsa dancing.

Next year, we're coming back, and we're going to bring you with us. Our parents know you well, and your folks know us, so it shouldn't be a problem.

Tomorrow we will be going ice-skating.
Goodnight, sweet dreams and see you when we return home,

Love,

Anastasia and Zophia ☺

The Dark History Behind Fantasium Hotel

By Larris Wade, Historian

Fantasium Hotel has always been described by many to be one of the most magnificent, opulent, and enchanting places to stay while on a week's holiday or a weekend break.

Before then, a small, simple, successful bed and breakfast named White Shells Guest House, owned by Mr and Mrs Greydeck stood in the very same place to welcome tourists, who ranged from humans to magic-wielding folk. All was going well, and the money was rolling in. The couple decided that, with all the money they took from their guests, they could build a sister bed and breakfast.

Then, one day, disaster struck.

A party of wizards, who introduced themselves as The Orgue Necromancers (pronounced Orj-you') came to stay. This was nothing sinister in itself, and they caused no trouble, until their chief offered Mr and Mrs Greydeck a substantial amount of money to try and buy the bed and breakfast from them.

The couple, who were humans without the use of magic, refused each time an offer was made, even though the leader stressed that Mr and Mrs Greydeck could work for them and earn a decent wage. Unfortunately for them, the wizards would not take no for an answer, and to show their displeasure, put a curse on the guesthouse. From then on, the number of tourists coming anywhere near them dropped significantly, and those who stayed found plenty to complain about, vowing that they would never return. There were leaks, floods, noisome smells, illness, rats and countless thefts. Worst of all, a fire ripped through the building one evening, killing Mr and Mrs Greydeck while they slept. The only lucky thing was that there were no guests staying there that fateful night.

As for The Orgue Necromancers, when it came to light that they were responsible for everything bad that had happened since their stay at White Shells Guest House, they were hanged for their use of curses and black magic to attack defenceless humans, and blatantly disobeying the Wizard and Witches Code of Conduct.

It was also discovered that Orgue was "rogue", with the letters muddled up – the real name for these evil-doers was Rogue Necromancers.

Since then, the remains of White Shells Guest House were destroyed and plans were made to put a bigger hotel in its place, which would be protected by good wizards, mages and anyone else who had knowledge of how to use defensive magic, and an invisible shield was put around the hotel that could detect and thwart anyone or anything with malicious intent and this defence system is still in use today. The ghosts of Mr and Mrs Greydeck wander round the hotel, offering friendly help and advice to staff and vacationers who can see and hear them, at Fantasium Hotel. They even assist in the cleaning of rooms and making the beds ready for the next visitors. All in all, every tourist is made welcome by staff both living and dead, magical and non-magical and many return every year to spend their holiday there.

Ballroom Dancers

(A poem found on a table in the ballroom of one of Fantastica's hotels. It is said that it was penned by a ghostly ballroom dancing couple. On the other hand, those who do not believe in the supernatural insist that it is the work of someone with a brilliant imagination and who just happened to get ideas from the mysterious sights they saw. Whoever wrote this piece, whether they be living or deceased has never come forward. The debate continues. One thing is agreed – there has never been any evidence to be found on CCTV).

As the magical folk, spirits of the four elements, and a few humans watch my partner and I perform our special dance that we both know and love so well

In the majestic ballroom we dance while classical music is played by elves and humans on instruments of gold bedecked with crystals

We both dance under the huge sparkling diamond
chandelier from which lit candles hang and star-like
lights wink and glitter on the ceiling

We dance from one ornate pillar to the others
All made from onyx and tower from floor to ceiling
While on the walls hang shimmering flowers

I dance with my partner upon the black glittering
floor while around us sit some magical folk on their
magic carpets
Others sit on platinum chairs with velvet cushions
with the humans

We make merry with the little folk and elementals,
The humans who have the gift to see us clearly join
in the ballroom dancing with us too

Thank you ghosts, the ballroom guests say, for
entertaining us all tonight and they escort us back to
the hotel we have been haunting for two hundred
years

Bedroom Window

(A poem created by a Fantastica resident named Lena who actually witnessed the events of which she has written. These are an annual phenomenon although it is unknown why they occur. Before writing this poem, Lena had been diagnosed with a life-threatening illness. At first, she was angry about how this could have happened to her, and in denial, until a close friend named Lainey suggested she used creative writing as a means of coping. Lena flatly refused, telling her friend there was no point, and that she was going to the afterlife soon anyway. This upset Lainey, and she left the hospital, according to witnesses. When she had calmed down, Lainey set about raising donations to help Lena recover and visited her as often as she could. One morning, and at different times that day, she and a nurse got her out of bed to see something spectacular out of the hospital window. It encouraged her creative juices to start flowing.

Since then, Lena has made a full recovery and is employed as a nurse).

Outside my bedroom window in the morning,

I see spectacular sights as the sun is dawning,

Like magic folk playing among the flowers

And multi-coloured rainy showers

Outside my bedroom window in the day

I see phantom children laugh and play,

Ghostly ships sail through rain

And disappear when the sun comes out again

Outside my bedroom window at evening time

I see sights so glorious and sublime

Like people walking on rivers of red

And children playing on a floating bed

Andrea Lightfoot

Outside my bedroom window at night

I see splendid sights of such delight

Like glowing rainbows that stretch so far

And luminous bubbles around our closest star

Behind the Door

Three children – Brody, Baylee and Laraine, played upstairs in the mansion in which they lived with their parents, butler and servants. Laraine busied herself with Solitaire, while her brother and sister played Chess.

After a while, one of the maids knocked at their door, then entered, carrying a tray with three glasses on top. She was a middle aged lady who had worked for the family for years.

'Excuse me Master Brody, Miss Baylee, Miss Laraine, I have brought refreshment for you - homemade lemonade if you please'. She took a glance out of the window. 'I daresay it's a nice day to play in the garden.'

'We'll go outside in a minute', Brody told her. The maid, whose name was Mrs Cartwright, nodded and bowed herself out. The children continued with their play. Soon, however, they grew bored, and the thought of going outside to play grew more and more appealing.

'Mother! Father! We're just going out to play in the garden!' Laraine yelled excitedly to their parents who sat conversing in the Sitting Room.

'Yes, it is a delightful day to do so', agreed their father, nodding.

The children hadn't been playing long, when Baylee suddenly noticed that there was a door in an oak tree close by. Naturally curious, in the way young children are, they went to investigate.

The mysterious door opened outwards to reveal stone steps that wound round in a spiral.

'Who's going first?' asked Baylee.

'You can,' offered Brody. 'You saw the door first'.

The children made their way up the staircase until they came to a circular room in which an elf sat mending shoes for a wizard. The aforesaid wizard stood over a smoky cauldron. Both looked up when they saw Brody, Baylee and Laraine.

'Ah, children! Do please come in and make yourselves comfortable', said the wizard. 'Gaivu, get the children some refreshment. Will hot milk and honey with cinnamon do?' This last part was addressed to the young mortals. They nodded. Gaivu made himself busy sorting drinks, while the wizard spoke to them.

'What spell are you making?' Brody asked curiously.

'I'm creating a magical musical box for King Oberon and Queen Titania,' he explained. 'They receive a gift for every year they are the rulers of Fairyland. Oh, and forgive me for not introducing myself. I am Wizard Susuas. Tell me your names'.

'I'm Brody and these are my sisters, Baylee and Laraine'. Gaivu handed them their hot drinks, and conversation began to flow.

What was it like living in the mansion? Did they go to school or did they have a governess? Could they play a musical instrument? Baylee explained that she was learning to play the clarinet, her brother played the trumpet, and Laraine was having singing lessons. Laraine opened her mouth to say something when someone else's voice floated up the stairs.

'Susuas! Have you got that musical box ready yet? I'll take it to Fairyland for you. Save you having to make the journey…..'

'Quick! In here!' Gaivu the elf hurried the bewildered youngsters into a round cupboard in the corner.

'Why do we need to hide?' asked Baylee.

'It's Jag, a goblin who hates children. He doesn't much care for human adults or teenagers, but he dislikes children even more', Gaivu whispered. He stayed in the cupboard with them. They huddled close to him, frightened. Gaivu himself was frightened for them. They had no defence against the goblin, unlike him.

'I haven't quite finished it yet, Jag. Besides, I don't mind making the journey to Fairyland. I do have other errands I need to run there too'.

'Yes, but at your time of life......'

'I wouldn't let a little thing like "my time of life" stop me', the wizard argued back.

'Don't mean to change the subject, but I'm sure I can smell children', Jag suddenly remarked.

'Just your imagination', Wizard Susuas replied, hoping and wishing the goblin would go away soon.

'No, I swear! Nasty, horrible, smelly little children! Can't you smell them? They smell dreadful!' The goblin began looking in every nook and cranny.

'You're wasting your time', pleaded Susuas. 'There's only me and Gaivu here! Why don't you go about your business elsewhere? Surely there's work you could be doing in Goblin Town?' The wizard, elf and children fervently hoped he wouldn't look in the cupboard. But he did and immediately saw Brody, Baylee and Laraine, who tried to hide behind Gaivu.

'Ah! So it was just my imagination was it?' 'Just you and Gaivu here is it? The goblin began to mutter sinister, ominous sounding words, while waving his hands about in theatrical fashion.

'Stop!' cried Gaivu. 'You can't just put a spell on innocent children! They've done nothing to you!'

'Silence, you piffling little elf!' barked the goblin. 'Or you'll be a stone statue too!'

Jag continued with his mutterings. He didn't get very far. A blinding flash of blue-white light, and the goblin had disappeared.

'Good riddance to bad rubbish', said Gaivu. 'I thought you were all goners just then'.

'You did well to put that disappearing spell on him when you did, Gaivu', the wizard remarked. 'Just one more line of that statue spell, and the children would have been in serious trouble'.

He went back to creating the musical box for the royal fairy couple while the children looked on. Gaivu got back to his shoe mending.

Then a voice familiar to the youngsters floated up to them.

'Brody! Baylee! Laraine! Time to come in for tea!'

They bid the wizard and elf farewell, and sped towards the mansion for their tea. They didn't mention their adventure behind the door in the tree. Nobody would have believed them anyway.

But they did become regular visitors there.

Calm inside the Bubble

(From 'The Great Tome of Relaxation', a meditation book kept in the Great Fantastica Library, built around the time of the Roman Empire. It was created by Anjali, a yoga teacher, who is originally from India, living and employed at one of Fantastica's Gymnasium and Leisure Centres. A special interview with Anjali follows this meditation, which has been reproduced by special permission)

You are lying inside a huge bubble, surrounded by the great outdoors.

Music plays softly, and it helps you to relax. Inch by inch the bubble rises up from the grassy floor, until it is about seven feet up. Then you are taken on a floating cruise.

You float over the tops of trees. There are children climbing one of them, and your eyes catch glimpses of fairy-folk and dryads every now and then. In return they watch as you pass by. The children point excitedly up at you.

You enter clouds then, and the domain of the sylphs. You gaze in wonder at the circular rainbow that you pass through. Sailing along the sky, and through clouds, you gaze in wonder at the magnificent palace in the sky.

The bubble slowly descends and you find yourself travelling through vales, and valleys, over hills and lakes and mountains, and through woodland. Throughout, you catch sight of salamanders, peri, merfolk, fairy-folk, and other elementals.

You float through a huge crystal cave, where the gnomes and dwarves stop their labours to watch you pass gently by.

Now you are floating over a flowery meadow, and it is isn't long until you are finally home and the bubble lands smoothly.

Once you are out, the bubble floats away to take someone else on a floating adventure.

An Interview with Anjali

By Levi Young, newspaper columnist for The Mage Chronicles

So, Anjali, tell us about your life in India

I grew up with my mother, father, brothers and sisters, in abject poverty, in one of the poorer parts of India. My parents could not afford to send myself or my siblings to school, and taught us what they knew at home. It also meant that we had to take low-paid, menial jobs as soon as we could.

What other hardships did you face?

Bullying and harassment, by people who were better off than ourselves. My siblings and I would sometimes bump into children whose parents could afford to send them to school and they would laugh and jeer at us, calling us names and throwing objects. We also faced illness and had to travel away from home just to find clean water.

How did you get to live and work in Fantastica?

I had been sent to work in the fields with my siblings, picking tea leaves. This was actually one of the better jobs I remember having, compared to some we had been forced to take on. Whilst we were there, one of my sisters noticed a door set into the ground and we set off to explore. In Fantastica, we met a yoga practitioner when we were sat at a table outside a café. He bought us each a drink and we got talking about how we could leave India and make a better life for ourselves here.

Did this yoga practitioner, or yogi, as they say, inspire you to become one yourself?

Pretty much, yes. He invited us, that is, my family and I, to his yogic sessions which we thoroughly enjoyed. I decided that I would like to teach yoga myself, while my siblings each had their own ambitions, like becoming a doctor or a mechanic or working in the science industry.

Each of us did have problems and drawbacks along the way of one sort or another, which were physically and emotionally draining, but we were encouraged by our friends and supporters never to give up and that a dream always comes true for those who really work for it.

Down Steps

(The events outlined below are regular occurrences in one of Fantastica's underground passageways, known as the 'Mystical Meander', and they inspired the yoga teacher who wrote 'Calm inside the Bubble' to also create this piece. It is sometimes used by yoga teachers in the last relaxation part of a yoga session).

You open a door, and find some stone steps. You close the door behind you and holding tight to the rail on the stone wall, make your descent. As you go, you see that the walls are adorned by tiles of glowing gentle colours of pink, blue, and white. You put a hand on a pink tile and find that you have left a blue handprint. You touch a blue tile and leave a white handprint. You touch a white tile and leave a pink handprint.

Then you move on down the steps and you leave the tiles behind. As you continue your descent, you see a rainbow in front of you. It never leaves your line of vision and seems to move downwards with you, until gradually it fades away to nothingness.

Then gentle pan-pipe music replaces the rainbow and you listen, soothed and relaxed as you go down these straight stone steps. As the pan-pipe music continues, you see that the walls are adorned with pictures of dolphins, and you see that the dolphins are moving, diving into the pictures of waves.

Eventually the pan-pipe music fades and the moving dolphins are left behind, and replaces by precious and semi-precious stones that sparkle and glitter. You pick a ruby, a sapphire and a topaz, and then you find a moonstone and a carnelian and put them in your pocket to take home.

Now as you travel down the steps, you see white candles, with their flames gently flickering, in little alcoves in the walls. Around the base of each candle there are red roses and spray carnations. You also notice that the flames change colour, from white, to yellow, to orange then red and back to white. You stop to rest and watch them. Then after a while you go on your way.

Now you've come to a flat piece of stony ground, and rest on the stone bench there against the wall.

There is more music, but this time it is the sound of an orchestra playing Brahms Lullaby. You close your eyes, sit back and listen to the soothing music. The music ends and you are ready to move on.

There is another door, and more steps, but this time they move upwards. As you ascend, you see that the grey uninteresting steps are turning into different colours of the rainbow and that the walls, now white and light pink, feel like cotton wool to your touch. Then the steps return to their former state, and the walls turn back to stone.

You carry on upwards and notice that at each side of the steps candles are glowing. Like the ones you saw before, their flames are changing colour, but these candles are gold and glittery. You take care to stay in the middle of the staircase, as not to knock the pretty candles over, and soon leave them behind.

Now mist is covering the walls and ceiling, and the only thing you can see are the steps, now covered in neon lights, and these guide you to a silver metallic door.

You step through and find yourself floating in mid-air. You have a feeling of peace and tranquillity. As you float, your mind runs through the wonderful things you have seen and heard. Right now you can hear the sounds of pan-pipes reaching your ears through the rainbow hued mist.

You begin to float slowly down one dark corridor, then down another one which is filled with soft light and thousands of bubbles. You soon discover that you are no longer surrounded by steps or walls, but by beautiful countryside.

You stand up, and head for home, guided by instinct. Once there, you run yourself a lovely hot bath and lie back and relax. When you get out, you wrap yourself in a large fluffy white towel to dry, then you put on your nightclothes and settle down in an armchair, next to merrily blazing coal fire.

Surely this was just a beautiful dream? You recall putting some precious and semi-precious stones in your pocket, just before you saw the candles with their colour changing flames, and you check your pockets.

You pick out the ruby, sapphire, topaz, moonstone, and carnelian and you gaze at them while holding them in the palms of your hands.

So you weren't dreaming.

The Discovery of 'The Mystical Meander'

For those who visit this charming, magical, bewitching passageway, it is hard to believe what it used to be like when it was first discovered in medieval times. Back then, Mystical Meander had not yet been named, and visitors there reported the place as dark, eerie, and like a tomb. There were also reports of malevolent spirits, and goblins, witches, and wizards who used it as a place to study and practice the dark arts.

There were skirmishes throughout the centuries, between those who followed the way of good, white magic, and those who dealt in bad, black magic, and more often than not, those who practised the dark arts, and followed the ways of evil, found themselves more powerful than their more benevolent counterparts. Mortality rates were alarmingly high on both sides, sadly more on the good side than the dark side. Eventually, people gave up fighting the evil, demonic forces to gain control of the passageway, leaving them to continue their habits of black magic.

Then, in the nineteenth century, a crusader whose name was Holger Ahlberg, came to Fantastica from his native Sweden. Word had got to him about the passageway and he came to join in the fight against those who dabbled in demonic sorcery. Under his command, his followers fought bravely against those who followed the ways of darkness and wickedness. Holger himself was captured by a small group of goblins, and was sentenced to death for his part in attempting to over-run the passageway, but was rescued by a fellow comrade just moments before he was due to face capital punishment.

The battle continued, and in Holger, the dark side met its match, driven back by the use of magical fire and lightning, by the good folk. When the wizards, witches, and goblins who traded in the magic of darkness were all killed in battle or executed, work began on exorcising the malevolent spirits. It was a pain-staking process and took months.

Then, with the last of the spirits banished, the passageway was imbued with protective magic and spells and was transformed into the captivating tourist attraction it is today.

There is a plaque just outside the entrance to Mystical Meander, in memory of those who fought and gave their lives for its liberation from the dark forces of evil, and a marble statue of Holger Ahlberg also stands there proudly.

Escapade

(This article is taken from 'The Mage Chronicles', a magazine produced exclusively for Fantastica residents. It was told to Zachary Denson, a feature writer for 'The Mage Chronicles', by Rob, a former student with dyslexia which affects the ability to read. He is currently an actor. Loren is a dressmaker and Wilton works as a Geography teacher. In their spare time, they often visit Old Witch Shadowcharm and her gnome companion, Froben).

Rob disliked school. When questioned why he had been absent, he had shrugged his shoulders and muttered how boring the lessons were, and how they never really learned anything anyway, so what was the point in going? When he did come to classes, he played the clown. Most of his peers thought he was hilarious, some of the more mature minded students would tell him to grow up and stop disrupting the class, and then there were a few who took absolutely no notice of Rob at all.

On this particular day, and at break time, he was playing football in the Lower Tier school yard with Wilton and Loren who also didn't care much for school either. Hearing the dreaded school bell summoning them back to lessons, Rob motioned towards a sizable hole in the hedge close by. It led into fields, and freedom from school.

'I've no idea where we're going,' Rob admitted to the others. 'But anywhere's better than that dump behind us'.

'I'm supposed to be in Textiles,' said Loren. 'Worst subject ever. I wouldn't even mind, but I can't even sew, and it's boring anyway.'

'I've got Geography,' Wilton told them. 'We've got this supply teacher who's absolutely useless. I could teach people the subject myself, and I'm a student'.

They had been talking while walking for a couple of miles now, and it was Loren who saw the little cottage first.

'It's probably some little old lady who lives there with her cat. Fancy doing knock and run?' she asked.

'Oh there's no need for that', said a voice behind them. The three students spun round to find a gnome standing there, tut tutting. 'Skiving off school! You'll never learn anything'.

'We don't learn anything anyway,' said Wilton. 'It's a waste of time going'.

The gnome looked at the schoolkids.

'You come in here with me. Old Witch Shadowcharm will sort you all out'.

The youngsters hesitated.

'Well? Come on then! She's not going to turn you into toads', said the gnome.

They reluctantly followed the little man inside, and saw a tall lady dressed in black sat in her rocking chair reading a book, her horn-rimmed glasses perched on the end of her hooked nose. She peered over them at the children.

'Thank you, Froben. Now children, I believe you should all be in lessons'.

They groaned. Was the witch going to cast a spell that would teleport them back to their dreaded classes? 'Why then, are you playing truant?'

'School's boring', Wilton volunteered. 'They don't teach us anything anyway'.

His schoolmates agreed.

'Well, you can't wander round aimlessly just because you don't like school or certain lessons', Old Witch Shadowcharm told them firmly. 'That's right, isn't it Froben?'

The gnome nodded. 'They could do their work here, if you look in your crystal ball and see what they're supposed to be studying'.

'Great idea', smiled Old Witch Shadowcharm. She peered closely inside her sparkling ball.

'Wilton, you have Geography,' she said matter-of-factly. 'It seems you have a supply teacher who does not know this subject well enough.' She waved her hands, and the room where Loren was meant to study Textiles appeared in the crystal ball. The teacher was ignoring the class, instead sitting with his feet up at his desk. Lastly, she turned to Rob.

'I see you have English,' she told him. 'I can't think why you are missing out on reading A Midsummer Night's Dream. It's one of William Shakespeare's masterpieces.'

Rob opened his mouth to speak. The witch held up her hand to silence him. Read this,' she ordered, handing over a book titled 'Rules of Being a White Witch'.

He stared at the page which had opened for him. 'I'm not reading that,' he said sharply. 'I…..'

The witch looked into her crystal ball again, and saw the words on the page how he saw them – blurred with letters running into each other.

'Ah! You're dyslexic! So that's why you play truant! You think your friends and teachers will laugh at you because you struggle to read words on a page or screen.'

She got up from her rocking chair and opened a cabinet.

'Here, take these magic glasses', she instructed Rob. 'They will help you make sense of what you read. Loren, take this magic needle for your Textiles lesson, and Wilton.' Old Witch Shadowcharm performed more hand waving over her precious ball. 'Your usual Geography teacher is on the mend and will back within a couple of days. You just need to persevere with your supply teacher for a little while longer. Take this ball to aid you.' She handed Wilton a small ball made of a soft material. Froben escorted the young trio back to school, then disappeared into thin air back to his mistress.

The teachers and students couldn't understand how Wilton managed to stay awake in Geography, or how Loren was suddenly able to sew, and sew really well, or how Rob was happy to read aloud to the class all of a sudden instead of playing the fool. Only the three of them knew that they had had help from a witch and a gnome, and it was a secret they would never tell. Sometimes after school, they would go and help Froben in the garden...

Festival of Dance

(Told by various people, interviewed by one of Fantastica's diarists. Celestine herself now teaches ballet, as well as folk and tap dance and has appeared in many theatre productions).

Celestine is excited about tonight. Nervous too, but mostly excited. Not many girls receive an invitation to dance for the royal couple, King Oberon and Queen Titania, in Fairyland, but Celestine has.

She will wear her shimmering pearly-white ballet dress with her white sparkly tights, and pale pink ballet shoes that were a birthday present from her grandmother who had once attended ballet lessons herself when she was younger. In her hair she will wear a pale pink rose, a real one, from the garden.

There will be a good many in attendance at the Festival of Dance in Fairyland. Not just the fairies, pixies, elves, dwarves, gnomes, brownies and other little folk, but also the elementals that represent Fire, Air, Water and Earth. Mermaids and mermen will watch from nearby lakes.

Celestine's own ballet tutor, Madame Lili Devereux will also be there to give support as will the whole of her ballet class.

Deities will also be there, some spectating from the ground, others from the branches of trees or from up in the sky. Goddesses such as Terpsikhore, the Greek Muse of choral song and dance, Greek warrior queen and goddess of the arts, Athena, along with Artemis, and Egyptian goddess Bast, the Celtic goddess Cerridwen, and Vesta, the Roman goddess of the sacred flame. Male deities will be God, Supreme Being of the Christians, and his Son, Jesus, along with Pan, the god of nature. Zeus will be in attendance along with his wife Hera. Apollo will also be there.

Ghosts of famous ballet dancers such as Margot Fonteyn will come to watch, as will retired ballerina Darcey Bussell, and the Philharmonic Orchestra will perform, to whose music Celestine will dance.

Last, but not least, her parents have been invited to witness their only child perform for an audience of magic-wielders, elementals, ghosts, merfolk, famous ballerinas, and immortals.

They are immensely proud of her, and the memories of this night will last forever.

An Interview with Celestine Goldsleeves

By Graciela Alfaro – The Mage Chronicles

How did it feel when you were chosen to dance for the fairy king and queen, the immortals and other non-humans, as well as famous professional ballerinas?

At first I was ecstatic, over the moon. It was an once-in-a-lifetime opportunity, and I couldn't wait to get home and tell my parents. When it sunk in who and what I was going to perform for, nervousness got mixed in with the excitement.

Did it mean you had to take on extra practice?

Apart from the usual Fridays, I had extra tuition on Wednesdays, and had to discipline myself to practice at home every evening after school, even though I had homework, and friends to hang out with.

What problems did you face when you found out you were the chosen student ballerina to

dance for the famous, magic-wielding, mythological and supernatural and so on?

I was told the wonderful news at the beginning of one of our sessions, surrounded by my fellow students. Most of them cheered, and congratulated me, wishing me the best of luck, but there were three girls who actually went on to bully me and do everything they could to force me to want to leave, and I would have left if I hadn't so much support from everyone else.

What kind of bullying did these girls mete out to you?

There was name-calling, which I could just ignore, and constantly being told I couldn't dance for toffee, and that I danced like an elephant. They would hide my things, and throw my bag around the changing room or dump the contents into a basin full of water, making me late for ballet class, and do whatever they could think of to upset me. They were later expelled from the Academy.

Have you seen your tormentors since your special performance?

Many times, and at first, they would completely ignore me, but as we grew up, they became more friendly, like they had been before. We're still in touch with each other. Dana, who was ringleader of the bullies, is now a distinguished composer, and her pieces are often played by bands and orchestras throughout Fantastica. Lilac is an artist, and Mina is a professional ice-skater. We meet up whenever we have the chance.

Glitter Cube

*(**From the diary of a Liverpool dweller, named Brenna, who lives within easy access to the mysterious land of Fantastica, kept at the Museum. She currently attends a course in the wielding of magic at one of Fantastica's colleges**).*

It is fun staying at Great Auntie Mary's in the school holidays. We both live in houses quite close to each other in Liverpool. There is a trapdoor in Great Auntie Mary's back garden that opens to a train station leading to the land of Fantastica.
Great Uncle Larsson is in Heaven, watching over her. He often visits. Sometimes he comes when I'm there and the three of us talk and play games. Occasionally he'll bring a couple of our ghostly ancestors with him and we'll have a game of Scrabble.

Great Auntie Mary grows a variety of fruits, vegetables and herbs and often makes her own tea.

For nettle tea she picks the leaves, puts them in a teapot and pours boiling water over them to remove their sting. She can also make dandelion tea, mint tea and a range of others.

She enjoys taking me to planetariums, zoos, adventure playgrounds, hands-on science experiment museums that are in Fantastica.

At night there are various things you can sleep in or on. There's no conventional bed. Who wants to sleep in a bed anyway? You can sleep in her garden den, or the tree house, a hammock, a cube, a giant marble…

Tonight I'm sleeping in a beautiful glitter cube. It's made of hard plastic. There are two layers of this afore-mentioned plastic and in between them is a water liquid with thousands of glittery particles floating about. There's enough room for three people. Great Auntie Mary is sleeping in a neon cube that constantly but gently changes colour. Great Uncle Larsson is keeping her company tonight. He bids me goodnight.

Inside the glitter cube I lie on pillows and have a blanket to keep me warm. In the lounge where the both cubes sit, music plays, soothing us to sleep.

The only one who is awake is my dead great uncle who watches over us as we slumber. The music can range each time I visit, from pan-pipes to Brahms Lullaby, to African tribal chants, Spanish folksongs………

Tonight we fall asleep listening to the native sounds of North American music.
I soon drift off, wondering what we will do tomorrow.

Letter by Brenna Grenville to a friend

Dear Angeliki,

Hope you're having a great holiday in Sweden. I've just been with my mum and dad, at my great auntie's house. We've been comforting her because she had an intruder. Whoever it was ransacked the place, took some things, and threatened my great auntie. She stood up to them, but she was quite shaken up. Luckily they didn't hurt her. Mum and Dad kept saying they should have been there with her, but my great auntie was saying there's no need, she had my great uncle to protect her. She told us it was only when the ghost of my great uncle appeared and threw objects at them, the burglar fled. I don't know whether the intruder could see my great uncle, or just an object lifting then flying by itself, but it got rid of him. Or her. By the way, I'm really sorry to be the bearer of bad news while you're sunning yourself abroad.

Anyway, we're cleaning up the mess (the burglar should do it, they're the one who trashed the place) and my great auntie has put a brave face on it, and decided she's going to buy some more herbs for the garden, and she's seen a glitter-cube and a neon colour-changing cube on Amazon, both of which you can sleep in, so she's going to order them for when I go to stay overnight. They're actually going to come from Fantastica, where they were manufactured. You and I visited there not so long age, remember? We could go again, when you've recovered from your holidays, if you like.

Mum reckons my great auntie should put some plants and herbs that protect against theft inside and around her home.

I'm going to get ready to go out with Nigel, Fraser, and Jessamine. We're going to the cinema to watch a sci-fi film, and are going to sit on the back row with popcorn and fizzy pop.

See you when you get back – don't get too sunburnt

Love,

Brenna x

Granny's Teapot and Other Strange Things in Her House

(A poem written by Crystal, a regular visitor to Fantastica. Her Grandmother – mentioned below – is a white witch, herbalist, and Fantastica dweller).

Granny has a strange teapot in her house

When you pour the tea out you can hear beautiful singing

Granny says it was a gift from a mermaid

She has a clock hanging on her kitchen wall

It only tells the hours of the day, one o'clock, two o'clock and so on

Granny says it's a gift from an elf

Granny grows herbs inside her house

Parsley, marjoram, nettle, fennel, basil, chives,
oregano and dill

She uses herbs when she makes her spells

My Granny's Unwanted Visitor

(By Crystal Madison)

I remember one night, when the lightning flashed periodically, and the thunder would follow his sister, and it was teeming down hard with rain. I was staying with my grandmother, who lives in Fantastica, as a treat. The cottage she dwells in was dark, except for the lit candles whose fidgety, dancing flames cast shadows upon the wall.

'Would you like a nice hot drink and some crumpets by the fireside?' Grandmother asked me.

'Yes please', I answered eagerly. I've always loved crumpets, especially when they're toasted on an open fire like my granny was going to do that night. We sat down upon cushions on the rug and she poured out tea for us both from her new pot, from which emitted beautiful singing. It made me think of mermaids and sirens of the seas.

'Where did you get your new teapot from, Gran?'

She told me about how she ventured onto one of Fantastica's beaches not so long ago, and how she met the mermaid who kindly gave it to her.

My grandmother had just rose to toast some more crumpets for us both, and she had opened her mouth to reply to my question of whether I should pour us both more tea, when the front door flew open and a goblin stood there, grinning at us wickedly. My heart sank, and I was thankful that my grandmother had the use of magic and could protect me if the need arose.

'Well! I say! This looks very cosy doesn't it?'

I didn't like his tone of voice, and from the look on her face, grandmother didn't either. It dripped with sarcasm.

'Perhaps you could go home, and help yourself to tea and crumpets there', she calmly suggested.

'Nah! You're alright. I'll stay here, in the warmth, while Great Mother Nature's throwing one of her temper tantrums outside.'

He chose a cushion to sit on and sat too close to me for comfort. He sensed my unease, and moved even closer to me.

'You can give my granddaughter some space. She doesn't need you right on top of her'.

'Oh, I'm not on top of her. I'm just sat next to her', and the goblin laughed, as if he had just made up the funniest joke in the world. Neither of us found him amusing.

The goblin didn't stay sat down for long. He got up and began to rifle through my grandmother's belongings.

'I would appreciate it if you stopped that', she told him firmly. 'If you want –'

'Oh my pesky, piffling, pixies! What a wonderful treasure!' the goblin exclaimed suddenly, picking up the teapot that a mermaid had once given my grandmother. Without even asking anyone else if they would like a drink, he picked up a dainty cup standing on the mantelpiece, and poured himself a cup of tea.

As he did so, his eyes widened in surprise and delight at the sound of the ethereal singing coming from the teapot.

'Come on, Grandma! Name a price for this!' the goblin ordered, waving the teapot round.

'The only price I'll name for you will be a price for you to leave us in peace', grandmother answered, 'and I'm not your grandma'.

'Just tell me how much this would cost, you doddery old woman', he snarled at her, his insolent demeanour now gone. He was towering over her. I was frozen in place, not daring to move and remind him I was present.

'Or you'll do what, exactly?'

I marvelled at how calm my grandmother was.

'I'll turn you into a frog. Or a cockroach. Or maybe a toad. That'll teach you a lesson'.

'How original. How about I turn you into a wombat?'

The goblin took this as an insult, and, throwing a hissy fit, started yelling a spell, pointing at my grandmother all the time. An electric-blue ball of flame danced in her hands, and I hoped she was getting ready to hurl it at the raging goblin. By now, Great Mother Nature had abated a little. The lightning and her brother, Thunder, seemed to have decided to call it a day, and only the falling rain remained.

Then my mobile phone played the tune that tells me I have received a text message, and the goblin stopped in his tracks, a horrified look on his face.

'Turn it off!' he ordered.

'Don't!' Grandmother put a hand out to stop me. The tune continued for a short while, then ceased. We both saw that the goblin had shrunk. I had an idea. I played a song that was also on my phone, and the goblin shrunk even more. He yelled at us to stop, and threatened to change us into every animal in existence. Grandmother put on a record, and the radio. Eventually, with all the music competing with each other, the goblin disappeared. Grandmother hugged me.

'To think that a non-magic human had the secret weapon to get rid of that goblin!' she laughed, and I laughed with her, both of us greatly relieved.

Gym Day

(*Eliza lives with her flatmates, Anna, Bethany and Niamh. Both she and Anna are employed at one of Fantastica's Gymnasium and Leisure Centres, while the others work in places outside the area. The article is featured in 'The Mage Chronicles', as an inspirational piece*).

I'd never been to the gym before. The very thought of going was nerve racking, and it wasn't helped by imagining that all sorts of people would be jeering at me. I mean, just try and imagine *me* in the gym, a chubby girl huffing and puffing on a treadmill, getting out of breath. I didn't want to join the gym but my doctor told me very sternly that I must go to the gym and exercise there at least four times a week. Four times a week?! . My doctor is one of those miserable old geezers who gives you lectures on how dangerous it is to be overweight and all the rest of it. Apart from that, I got fed up with bullies shouting fat-person-insults at me across the road then legging it, or shouting nasty things from their cars. People are so stupid. It's not as if I could run after them.

If I'm to be honest, though, the gym wasn't really all that bad. Yes, I felt really nervous when I met Jake, my instructor. What if he looked at me and only judged me on my size instead of getting to know me as a person? Lots of people did that. 'Erm, I'm Eliza,' I muttered, feeling myself go red, as he introduced himself.

'It's okay,' said Jake, who's voice calmed me somewhat, "I've seen it all before, and there are people who come here who are larger than you are. You've taken the hardest step already, just coming in here." Larger than me?!

He showed me how to use some of the equipment, and I saw people similar to me – people who needed to lose a few pounds, so even though I did notice slimmer people staring at me, at least I could take a little comfort in the fact that I wasn't the only chubby person there. Strangely, I even made friends with someone the first day I was there, which helped a lot. Anna, her name was. She'd been on the treadmill next to mine, and we had sort of got talking, though I was doing a lot of puffing and panting, (and sweating while I was at it).

She had a nice healthy figure and I dreamed of looking nice like that, and perhaps getting a new hairdo. Mine just looked dreadful.

The next session I had arrived at the gym, I got changed and had a chat with Anna in the cafe next to the gym. Then we had gone into the gym area, with our bottles of water and made a bee line for the treadmills and it was while we were jogging (Anna jogging, me trying to) when things got exciting.

Let me first tell you what the décor of the gym looked like. As a rule, the carpet was red, the walls were white, with pictures of famous athletes on them, and there were televisions in front of you. We were watching You've Been Framed when it suddenly went dark, and there were stars and planets racing by us in the opposite direction. We passed all the planets, from Mercury, all the way to Neptune, and passed Pluto, which had lost its planet status. This was really weird. Did *you* know Pluto isn't counted as a planet anymore? Well you do now. Comets shot by, and disappeared from view. There was nobody else apart from me and Anna.

I had turned to Anna, amazed. Where was everyone? 'Have you noticed, or is it me being stupid, or are we really going through space?' So I wasn't just imagining it. Anna was experiencing the same thing! It was a relief to know I wasn't turning into a nutcase.

'I did notice, yes. But I didn't say anything, in case you thought the heat was getting to me or something. Though I'm glad you mentioned it. I wouldn't have dared, for fear of being laughed at. I thought it was just me imagining things.' Mental sigh of relief. Almost as soon as it had started, the space travel was over and the room returned to normal. We then went on the rowing machines and played this game where your fish gets points for eating other fish, but loses points if it's eaten by a shark. Jake smiled and nodded at us. We must have seemed ok. Then the room changed again This time Anna and I were on the River Thames, London (not the River Thames on the planet Mardayaz, hundreds and thousands of light-years from Earth), and drawing quite a crowd, simply because we were on a floating rowing machine, and other river users were in boats. People took pictures. I cringed. I hated having my photo taken.

'Don't worry,' said Anna. 'I don't like having my photo taken either.'

'At least you've got a nice figure and a pretty face,' I replied.

'You've got a pretty face too, you know,' Anna tried to comfort me, 'and if you keep coming to the gym and eating healthily, then you'll have a beautiful figure like mine.' We both laughed. I wanted to have a figure like hers, no matter how long it took, though the sooner it happened the better. While I fantasised for the zillionth time about having a lovely slim figure it took me a little while to realise we were back in the gym. We headed for the exercise bikes, which I felt were less strain on the legs than the treadmill. Then we found ourselves, I know not how, equipped with helmets and knee protectors, on proper bikes (like you see cyclists using at the Olympic Games), both part of an international race. This time we were in the French Alps. We raced uphill, downhill, and whatever other way there was to cycle on the mountains, as people cheered us on. Caught up in the event, there was no way we could get away, and it was easier just to ride along with the thousands of other cyclists.

In the end, someone from Spain won the cycling race, and it was quite nice really to see the trophy in her hand and a look of joy on her face. An African person came second. However I did admit to Anna that I would have loved either her or me to have won it. We came last.

"Our folks would have been so proud of us," she smiled. "But then, they would have wondered how we managed to get into the race in the first place. Those people are the best cyclists in the world." No sooner had she spoken that we ended up back in the gym again. 'I don't know about you, Eliza, but I've had enough surprises today to last a lifetime. I'm getting changed, and then I'm going to Adele's Coffee Bar for lunch. Coming?'

I never told Mum about what exciting things happened at the gym. She wouldn't have believed me. The story, though true, is too surreal. But she was pleased to find that I'd enjoyed going, and even more so to find that I had made a friend.

Recently, I discovered that I'd lost some weight, and treated myself to new fashionable clothes and got my hair cut into a nicer, more flattering style. Anna came with me.

"You look absolutely lovely," she told me later, and we hugged. We moved in to a new flat together, along with a friend of hers and a friend of mine. Bethany, her name was. We had known each other for ages and she would always stand up for me against the bullies. When I told her about my new friend, she wanted to meet Anna as soon as possible. That was the thing with Bethany. She liked meeting new people. Anna's friend was Niamh, and she turned out to be pretty nice to, though she was quieter and a bit more reserved than Anna or Bethany.

'Anyone fancy coming to the gym and then ten pin bowling later?' Anna asked the three of us one evening.

You'd never seen people move so fast.

My Story – Before the Gym

By Eliza Onor

Ever since I started coming to the gym with my flatmate, Anna, where we are now both employed, people have been doing double-takes to see if it really is me they see before their very eyes. I am still no stick figure, but neither am I a "fat blob" (my bullies words, not mine). Instead, I am happy with my body shape.

I put quite a bit of weight on in high school and was tormented for my size, leading me to comfort eating. It also meant I was a loner. How I longed for the day I could leave school, and never return!

My hair and clothes weren't exactly pin-up pop-starlet criteria either. I looked, with my hair all permed, like someone from the nineteen-eighties. My clothes looked as though I had bought them from a shop aimed at the older generation. As you can imagine, I was totally unfit and did everything I could to get out of doing P.E or any sports at all at school.

There was something else too. Carrying so much weight around meant I got out of breath just climbing one flight of stairs. I always used the lifts at school, and anywhere else I went too.

Don't think, however, that I didn't want change. The taunts and the strange looks got to be too much. I wanted to look nice, and wear pretty, trendy clothes, and have a decent hairstyle, but I made up all sorts of excuses for myself. Looking back now, I think I wanted change, but was too scared to take the first step. Until one day, I paid a visit to the doctor for a routine check-up. He didn't speak much as he examined me, until he was sat back at his desk, me facing him.

'The term "early grave" comes to mind', he warned me ominously, and went on to dish out the so-called hard-hitting advice given to people who smoke, drink, and rock-and-roll. Most doctors I ignored, this one could count himself lucky – he was the only one I took notice of. I don't know how or why, there was just something about him that made me sit up and take notice, so to speak.

On the day I bit the bullet, so to speak, and went to catch the bus to the leisure centre. I had the misfortune of coming face to face with a few of my enemies, who treated me mercilessly. It shook me up, and, close to tears, I nearly turned and walked back home. It took all my resolve to stay at the bus stop. Then, at the gym, I saw fit, toned, healthy people. I was sure they were all staring, laughing and whispering about me. Again, I nearly turned back. I think the only thing that stopped me was the sight of a couple of other "big girls".

Today, even now, I'm glad I didn't. My courage to join the gym bought me not just new, trendy, stylish attire, and a fashionable hairdo, but most important of all, it bought me the opportunity to make friends and help transform people's lives, just like mine had been.

In my Dreams

(The creator of this piece of literature may have been inspired by what happens when anyone visits the ancient passageway mentioned in the third verse. It is just one of many found in Fantastica, and is known as the 'Passageway of Peace'. It remains a mystery as to who wrote it and when).

A red box glitters.
In my dreams I am taking it apart.
Metallic-red liquid flows forth and I find myself in a boat on that liquid travelling into an orange sunset.

The sunset turns into orange silk curtains.
I pull them and see a bounteous garden.
In my dreams I explore it.
I walk along the path till I come to the garden gate.

Now I am in a passageway bedecked with painted murals. Down the stony stairs I tread till I encounter a wooden door. I open it and fall into the air. I am in darkness, I am in mid-air, and as I float, I hear the gentle music from a harp, soothing me to sleep.

Mysterious Dream

(*A vivid, prophetic dream, recorded by a wise man of Fantastica as he sits beside gifted psychic, Toyanna, at her bedside. Whether the occurrences in this vision have come true or not have not yet come to light, and the meaning of the vision has not been revealed. Additional reporting is by an anonymous reporter*).

She's walking along a passageway. The floor is a glittery white, and the tiled walls are a polished pink and silver. Along these walls are mirrors, each showing not her reflection, as would be expected, but beautiful landscapes found all over the world. The door is at the end. It opens, showing rolling, sky-blue mist and blue lights that flicker like candle flames. The dreamer feels calm and relaxed but vaguely wonders why she is wearing a dress. She doesn't even wear dresses!

The dream has changed. She can't see herself now but observes the ghost of an old woman sitting at a low wooden table surrounded by Native Americans.

Her hair is silver rather than grey and is worn in a long plait. There are only a few wrinkles on her face. In front of her, in a hole in the table, a fire burns, its glow lighting the faces of the people around it. The Native Americans appear not to be able to see the ghostly lady, for they do not talk to her. The old lady is smiling, as if she approves of what the Native Americans say. They are telling stories of their "dreamtime legends".

Now the dreamer can see herself again and can see, as well, a pretty young maiden with flowing red curls down to her waist standing at the platform of a train station. Who is this redheaded girl? Nobody she can think of that she has ever met. In the dream, the train station could be anywhere. It does not occur to her to look for any signs that would tell her what train station she is standing at. A train rushes through, a blur of many colours, and then disappears. So does the girl. Could have asked her who she was.

There's another change of scene. She's holding the hands of a little boy and girl, and they are looking down a pitch-black hole.

The hole is dark, but a man plays a haunting tune on a cello. If only she could stay here forever, the music is so hypnotic and therapeutic. There is a rainbow, spilling colours into the starry night sky.

Then all this vanishes, and as if told to by an invisible person, all three look up at the sky. They are surrounded by nebulae, and they can see a star here and there twinkling through the clouds. The dream-children disappear and she is left alone, but once again she is invisible to herself. Who were these children, she wonders, and why didn't she ask them who they were when she had the chance?

Invisibility still cloaks her, but she can now see a teenage girl lying on her back on the grass, looking up at the fairy toadstool houses and the tall trees surrounding her. Another person that is unrecognisable. She sees fairy-folk flitting among the tall grasses and around the girl and in the sky. Her heart takes a leap as she sees something very few people do. Nobody sees her.

Just as she decides to ask the dream-teenager who she is, the youth and fairy-folk disappear, to be replaced by another vision.

The dreamer stands on rocks, visible to herself again. There, seen among the roaring turquoise waves of the sea are fish, dolphins, and mermaids, whose beautiful haunting melodies seem to lift her spirits. Mermaids! Her heart takes another excited leap.

Very few people have seen fairies, and even fewer have seen mermaids, unless they are believers in these mythological beings, whether they live in Fantastica or not.

Then she is somewhere looking down from the sky. It gives her a feeling of elation. The wind howls and shakes the trees of a dream-forest where nothing but weeds, nettles, and brambles are growing. She is glad to be above out of the gales way. A dream fire tears through the forest, the wind pushing it and howling its encouragement, where the tall trees block out the light, making it dark and dismal.

As the forest fire travels rapidly through the sinister looking woodland the forest changes. Trees fall, allowing younger, smaller plants to grow, the nettles, weeds and brambles are destroyed, and flowers and other plants sprout in their place, and the forest is lit up, as the rays of sunshine finally penetrate, and a rainbow shines over the treetops. A smile lights up the dreamers' face, as if she is a person who knows that good has triumphed over evil.

Toyanna wakes to see familiar faces at her bedside. She looks up at her parents, and her brother who look puzzled and a wise man who has been studying her while she has slept.

"Take heed. These dreams tell us of the future," *says the wise man. He leaves them to wonder what he means.*

The Tale of Witch Nightfear

(*By Larris Wade, historian*)

Way back in medieval times, there was a witch whose name was Nightfear, who dwelt in Fantastica. Many witches, like most of the ones in the present day, were good folk, with kind hearts and a love for music and dancing. Nightfear, on the other hand, was of the sort that dabbled in black magic, hexes, and curses. Her speciality was giving people nightmares. If anyone did her wrong, it didn't matter whether they apologised or not – that same night they would be plagued with bad dreams and nightmares.

These sinister visions were more vivid, so much so, that they led many of Nightfear's victims to take their own lives, while others were left as quivering wrecks. Nightfear would rub her hands in glee at the effect her spells were having on those on whom she was getting revenge. Some of them turned up at her cottage and begged the witch to take off the curse, and that they humbly apologised for any wrong they had caused her.

She laughed in their faces, and sent them away, to beg someone else to rescue them from their plight.

Once word got round, however, people started to avoid Nightfear like the plague, and would carry lucky stones, and talismans, around with them, to ward off black magic, for just in case they came face to face with her. Behind her back, people made the sign of protection, or hurried into their homes, locking the door behind them.

It happened that the Lord Mayor of Fantastica's son, Milton, was on his way to university one day. He was late, and shoved past her impatiently, telling her to "move out of the way, you dozy old crone", then started running. He was half an hour late for lectures, which displeased his tutor. Unknown to him, Nightfear was even more irate than the tutor at the way Milton had been so disrespectful to her and that night, he suffered horrible nightmares, not just on one night, but for a whole week, until his parents became suspicious. The finger of blame was pointed at Witch Nightfear. His father sent spies to observe her, while his mother admonished Milton for his rudeness to the witch.

The spies discovered exactly how she created her bad-dream and nightmares spells and when they had gathered enough evidence, they enticed her out of her cottage, and dragged her, bound and gagged through the streets of medieval Fantastica. People threw stones, rotten tomatoes and worm-ridden apples at her, and hurled insults. Eventually, she was tied to a chair, and lowered into a dark, deep lake, but was not brought back up.

It is said her ghost still haunts that lake, however most, except those of a wicked, malevolent nature, avoid the area.

New House

(*Both the buyer of this house and the estate agent were interviewed for this article which appears in a brochure aimed at advising potential customers who may want to purchase a house in Fantastica. The conversation between the two parties has been recorded and published with special permission*).

Now this is a new house, just built a couple of weeks ago. Let me show you around.

Sure.

First of all, this is the hall –

It's a lot bigger than the other hall. It's funny – it's just an ordinary detached house although the hall looks like one of those you'd find in a mansion! Oh sorry, I shouldn't interrupt.

It is okay, and you're right, the hall is like one you'd find in mansion, and there are winding stairs over there. I'll take you upstairs in a minute. Follow me and I'll show you the living room. Ah, here we are.

It's very unusual isn't it? Floating cushions, futuristic fireplace on the wall, and those lights on the ceiling are just like real stars!

Yes, they have the same twinkling effect. Of course, apart from what you've just pointed out, there are also ordinary things such as a chest of drawers here and a big bookcase, but as you can see, both of these are silver to match the fireplace.

What's this interesting looking contraption in the middle of the floor?

This is a Multi-Use Console. Let me show you. Basically you can listen to music, so you can put tapes, CD's, DVDs, etc. in here, and plug MP players and I-Pods in here, there's a computer, photocopier and scanner, so you can work from home if you wanted to, and there's also a plasma screen TV on the wall up there.

Through this door here, you have a little cinema that has a bar with popcorn and drink facilities. There are also plenty of cinemas throughout Fantastica that offer reasonable prices.

What's through this door here?

Follow me and I'll show you. See? This is the dining room and kitchen, both quite contemporary and spacious.

I like this big rug that's been put down, and oh, picnic benches and trees everywhere! I suppose you could have a picnic in here if it was nasty weather outside.

Yes, you certainly could, and you wouldn't get sunburned or bitten by horrible midges either.

I don't suppose you'd get fresh air, would you?

Actually you would. Just press this button here on the wall and see? Air conditioning! Or you could open a window or two.

What about the back garden? I'd like to have a look at that.

I'll show you the back garden last. First, let's go upstairs.

This is the master bedroom and as you can see, it's a pretty garden with a family sized tent in it.

So there's two gardens outside (front and back), one in the dining room, and one in here?

Exactly. Shall I show you the tent? Well, as you can see, that's where you sleep, and there's plenty of room for more than two people. Over here, and here as well, there are cupboards for your personal belongings. Now we'll go into the next bedroom.

Wow, it's like an indoor adventure play area!

Yes, you're right, it is. You can sleep wherever you feel like in here, in this tunnel, in these big plastic cubes, in this tent under the slide, anywhere at all.

Well it would make a change from sleeping in a bed anyway.

Yes, beds can be pretty boring, can't they? Comfortable, but boring. At least in here you can sleep in or on something different.

Okay. This is the art gallery, complete with everything you need for creative crafts and so on, and just down here is the planetarium. Don't forget, like the cinema we looked at before, there are also planetariums and art galleries in Fantastica, most of which are free. The ones which aren't often have offers for discounts on, so keep an eye out for those. Right. I'll show you the next bedroom.

Oh, it's a space bedroom.

Yes, you're right, it is, and you'd be sleeping in a floating bed, while stars, moons and planets whizz by. Another thing – see how everything in this room is floating – like the wardrobe, bookcase and beside table.

Oh yes! Just like in real space. So if we go into this room, we'll float too?

We would, yes. Fancy trying it?

This is cool! I'm actually defying gravity! Just wait till I tell my friends and family I have a room I can float in!

Rooms that allow you to float or fly are quite common in Fantastica. I've never known them to be anywhere else, save for Fairyland.
Anyway, if you follow me to the bedroom door, we'll be able to put our feet on the ground again and I'll show you the back garden.

I say, I like the garden! Much better than the one I've got at the house I'm living in at the moment.
You'll find that every time you look or come out into it, the garden looks different. Well, that's all I have to show you, I'm afraid. Have you any questions?

Well, it's such a lovely, unusual house, how much does it cost?

Five pearls, one jade and a gift for the fairy folk.

New Neighbours

(A letter from Lucy, when she and her family came to live in Fantastica. She works as an Environmental Health Agent alongside other humans, as well as gnomes, dwarves and earth spirits).

Dear Lucy,

I hope that this letter finds you well. My family and I met our new neighbours yesterday, when we moved house to go and live in Fantastica. You'll know that where we lived previously was a run-down, crime-ridden area where the unemployment rate was high. You've seen for yourself the yobs hanging around, in groups, looking and acting intimidating, and the other undesirables who we took pains to avoid. None of us ever dared to venture out alone. You've seen our own house have its windows broken, and graffiti sprayed onto the walls. That was bad enough, but our car was set alight yesterday. It was the final straw.

How thankful I am, and the rest of the family, that recently we discovered a door almost completely hidden in the long grass in what was a feeble excuse for a front garden. Deciding to investigate, we came across somewhere called Fantastica. It's quite a strange yet beautiful place. We returned to our own house to pack our belongings and move to Fantastica instead. The people who live next door seem to be very nice, polite and sociable people, and rather unusual too, you know. We found out they aren't your usual run-of-the-mill type of neighbour when they invited us into their house for a chat. Let me tell you a few things about them. I'm sure you'd be interested. They're a family of four like ours.

The first person I'd like to tell you about is the father, Jerome. He's a wizard, originally from Britain, and is one of the youngest members, believe it or not, of the British Wizardry Association. He's in his forties, and told us the oldest member is over few thousand years old. You wouldn't think, just by looking at him that he's a wizard, but he showed us his magic staff and did all sorts of clever tricks with it. He made things disappear and re-appear, float and change colour.

There is also an organisation called the International Wizardry Association which has members from all over the world. On August of each year, wizards from every country come together to compete for the Wizard of the Year Award, a spectacular huge gold trophy, adorned with sparkling stars. Like the Olympics, Paralympics, and Commonwealth Games, each country takes turns at being the host. Last year Jerome went to Switzerland and he won the trophy which he proudly showed us.

The mother is called Arielle and she's also in her forties. She sells things called Amulets of Protection, which she started creating after an incident that occurred when I was a baby. I've attached the story, which I obtained from the History section at a library in Fantastica, to this letter. We were shown some of her stock, and Arielle was happy to sell a few amulets to us for five pounds, or whatever we could give as payment. They were some of the most exquisite things I had ever seen. I've bought you one too. I hope you like it.

Arielle told us that the amulets protect their wearer from bad luck, curses, nightmares and evil spirits. They come in all sorts of colours too.

The shop where Arielle sells her jewels is called the 'Boutique of Protective Amulets' and before any customers come in, Arielle and a trio of white witches (witches who practise good magic) cast spells to allow the amulets to do their job and to bless these jewels and their wearer.

Then there's Hainos, the son, who is a magical performer, often working alongside his father, Jerome. In front of my very eyes, Jerome made a fire appear, and Hainos just walked calmly through it. Then he showed us how he can walk through a huge block of ice. Then he melted metal with his bare hands. Then he and Jerome both waved wands and created a fabulous indoor firework display. Hainos is twenty-two by the way.

Last of all, there is the daughter, the youngest in the family at twenty. Andromeda is a planetary ambassador.

She represents Earth, our planet, and her full job title is Planetary Ambassador of Earth. Hers is an exciting job.

Meetings are held on the High Planet that Andromeda and the other planetary ambassadors have to attend. She travels to different planets and galaxies, teaching other beings about Earth, learning about their cultures and ways of life and engaging in peace talks with them.

She often stays at the homes of her fellow ambassadors who are beings from other planets. (Each planet has its own ambassadors). Arielle told me that Andromeda is, at present, staying at the home of Zedah, a female alien, and her family. Zedah is the planetary ambassador of Zetra, a planet many galaxies from ours. The Zetrans are a humanoid race, very friendly and peace loving, but they put up a good fight if and when any hostile races try to invade. They eat the same kind of food we do here, and are basically just humans like us, except they live on a distant planet. I wouldn't mind sleeping in the kind of bed Andromeda sleeps in when she's there like she is now.

It's a big bubble, heated inside so it's nice and warm, so no blankets are needed. Arielle said that we will meet Andromeda and Zedah very soon.

Well, that's all I've got to tell you, except I've started collecting crystals and gemstones. I've got a rose quartz and an amethyst so far which Arielle has given me.

Anyway, take care of yourself, and I shall see you soon

With lots of love and fairy dust,

From

Ayesha x

The Sorcerer

(By Arielle's daughter, Andromeda)

My mother, Arielle, is the owner of the 'Boutique of Protective Amulets' which is what she has been for a number of years, and it all came about after a terrifying encounter with a black-magic practising sorcerer.

I was born on a day of fair weather. The sun shone brightly, children played outside, and the birds sang in the trees. It stayed like that for a week. My father Jerome had stayed at home with my mother to help raise me, and my older brother Hainos helped out too, when he wasn't performing magic at public displays.

On the Saturday after, black, heavy, ominous clouds rolled over Fantastica, and Sister Lightning and Brother Thunder made their presence known. No-one thought anything of it. Storms were, and are, no more unusual in Fantastica than anywhere else.

I can imagine that some people probably looked up at the sky and muttered,

"Oh, there's a storm brewing," and left it at that, knowing that Great Mother Nature would eventually calm down.

Someone knocked on our door, and my mother opened it, thinking that it was one of our family – there was only her at home with me, you see. Instead, a tall dark figure, illuminated by Sister Lightning, pushed past her aggressively.

'Well? No husband to protect you and the baby?'

His tone was cold and mocking.

'What do you want?'

My mother answered back in a voice as cold as his, trying to show that she was not afraid of him. I must have sensed that something wasn't right, and I began to whimper. Mother picked me up and held me close.

'That's a beautiful baby you have there. What's her name?'

'Andromeda,' she answered tersely. 'What are you here for?'

She knew he wasn't really interested. It was only to soften her up, and it vexed him that it didn't work. He leaned very close to her, and gripped her chin in a way that was meant to be intimidating rather than intimate, and lifted it up so she was forced to look at him.

'I don't like the way you speak to me', he told her, his voice dangerously quiet. 'You need to learn your place, woman. Now, if you hand me the baby, I can bring her up and she can study the art of black magic, and become my assistant. I will see to it that she has a good life and will want for nothing, as well as learning worthwhile skills'.

My mother angrily shook herself free.

'Why should I give my daughter to someone who is evil as you? There is no way I would give any of my offspring away to one who practises black magic!'

The sorcerer was taken aback at first, but he managed to get my mother away from me, and myself into his arms in a manner so fast, she didn't realise what was happening, and when it dawned on her, it was too late. He had used a spell on her. Then he left, with me wailing, into the stormy night.

I don't remember anything. All that I related has been what I have learnt through Arielle, other members of my family, and witnesses from homes nearby.

I had been left in a basket upon a large rock not far from land. The sorcerer was nowhere to be seen, but his dark magic was strongly present. Every time someone attempted to save me, they either drowned, even those who were adept swimmers, or were eaten by sharks or sea-monsters. Some of my would-be heroes (and heroines) did not have the use of magic, and those that did, found out the hard way that the sorcerers' was stronger than theirs.

Then Hainos came. My brother, Hainos and my father Jerome.

Arielle hadn't been too happy at first. Others who have gone before you have perished, she told them worriedly. My father put a comforting arm around her and told her that she knew how powerful they were as individuals. Together, they would be even more so. They were right. The sorcerer's dark magic was no match for the good, white magic wielded by my father and brother.

There were parties and celebrations when I returned home to Fantastica, and my family were reunited. My mother summoned the goddess of vengeance, Nemesis, to find the evil sorcerer and bring him to justice. No one knows what happened to him, but to this day, he has never been found.

After the last celebratory bonfire had died down, and people had gone home, three white witches approached Arielle and told her they could create a protective amulet for our home, free of charge, and shook their heads when she offered to pay them. Also, how could she return their kindness?

'It's from the goodness of our hearts,' they told her. 'If you really want to repay us, you would do well to open a shop and allow us to work alongside you as your assistants'.

My mother was interested, and she talked at length with the witches, and so, with their help, and the support from my father Jerome and brother Hainos, a shop called 'Boutique of Protective Amulets' came into being, and is still helping customers from near and far to protective themselves, and others, from the forces of malevolence.

One day, both I and Hainos will inherit it. It is something we both look forward to.

Obsidian Stone

*(**Recorded by one of Fantastica's diarists who interviewed college students, Rosalie and Carran, as well as Tobrien, a brownie, for his book Life in Fantastica**).*

Like everyone else at the end of a busy day at college, sociology student Rosalie was heading off home. The college bus, filled with students, passed her as she walked. With her, chatting animatedly on his mobile to one of his friends, was her engineering student brother, Carran.

They were walking through the park, when Rosalie suddenly heard a voice from the large blackberry bushes on their left.

'Oh come on!' it moaned impatiently. 'It's got to be here somewhere! It can't just have vanished into thin air!'

Curious, Rosalie went to find out what it was that had to be there somewhere. Carran rang off from his mobile.

'Where are you going, Ros? Home's this way, not through the bushes'.

'Someone's lost something, so I'm going to help', she answered her brother. Behind the blackberry bushes she saw what appeared to be a gnome or a dwarf.

'Wow! A little garden gnome!' exclaimed Carran when he came face-to-face with the little man, whose attire was quite scruffy and tramp-like.

'If it's all the same to you, lad, I'm a brownie'.

'What have you lost? We'll help you find it if you like', offered Rosalie. 'I'm Rosalie, and this is my brother, Carran', she added.

'It's my obsidian stone', explained the brownie, 'and I'm Tobrien. I do the gardening in this park, alongside the humans and members of other races. I had the stone in my pocket, to give to my wife later. I was going to take it to the elven jeweller who has his shop under one of the apple trees in this park so he could put a gold chain through it.'

'You wanted to give your wife an obsidian necklace?' Rosalie asked.

'Yes, that's right,' Tobrien nodded. 'It's our wedding anniversary tomorrow. We've been married for two hundred years.'

'Two hundred years?' gasped Carran. He and his sibling exchanged glances.

Tobrien made a dismissive gesture.

'Ah! That's nothing! My wife and I know folks who have been married for years more than that! Anyway, enough talking, let's get looking shall we?'

'Couldn't we get a group of people to help us?' suggested Carran. 'It might be better than just three pairs of eyes looking for your stone'.

Tobrien thought for a moment.

'Not a bad idea actually', he agreed. 'The missus is out for a day away from here with a couple of our fairy friends anyway and won't be back for some time, I should hope. So yes, by all means, let's go and round up some helpers'.

Soon, the trio of two humans and one brownie were joined by fairy-folk, other brownies, dryads, dwarves, gnomes, and members of other races, all eager to lend a helping hand to their friend Tobrien. The only individual who refused point-blank, and quite belligerently, was a goblin who lived in a small cave surrounded by oak trees.

'But then, what do you expect? He's a goblin', remarked Tobrien to Carran and Rosalie after the ill-mannered creature had grouched and grumbled, and told them to go and jump in the pond.

'Thanks very much for your help. Much appreciated,' the brownie had remarked ironically to the goblin before turning away from him. The college students followed suit. The goblin shouted something quite uncouth at their receding backs. Creatures of other races stepped forward and around the trio, blocking them from view.

'I'm just going to ring our mum,' Rosalie told Tobrien, 'and let her know we're going to be a bit late getting home. She gets a bit worried if we don't let her know we're staying out.'

Ears pricked up to hear what the young female human was saying into her mobile device.

'One of our mates' dad has bought this present for his wife because it's their anniversary soon', they all heard her say. 'But he's dropped it somewhere in the park and we're going to help look.'

'Well, that's kind of you,' a female voice was heard to say from the phone, 'but I'm sure there must be other people who could help him look, or he could get her...'

'Yes, but we promised. So we'll get something from the chippy later, save us having to cook anything when we get home'. She stole a questioning glance at Carran, who nodded.

She rung off.

'Our mates' dad, eh?' Tobrien queried, eyebrows raised.

'I couldn't really say we were going to help a brownie,' explained Rosalie. 'She probably wouldn't believe us'.

'Adults don't believe anything they don't see with their eyes half the time. At least a lot of them don't, and any adult humans who believe in the fairy, brownie, elven, and whatnot folk get laughed at, poor things. You both obviously believe in us, otherwise you wouldn't be able to see us.'

'As for getting something from this "chippy" place, which I understand is human slang for a fish and chip shop, you can both come to my place, and I'll cook up something nice for the two of you'.

'Won't your wife be home then?' asked Carran. 'She might wonder why you've invited us home'.

'Oh, I didn't think of that'.

The brownie looked crestfallen, but quickly cheered up.

'Leave it to me'.

Everyone who was willing to help searched for the obsidian stone. No fallen tree, bush or shrub leaf was left unturned, and they were checked underneath every pebble too.

The goblin emerged, scowling, from his den.

'Aren't you going to help, goblin?' one of the elves called after him as he skulked away. He spun round to where the voice was coming from.

'Go and turn yourself into a cockroach and crawl under a stone, elf', the goblin told him ill-manneredly.

The elf, unperturbed, smiled sweetly.

'Certainly! I'll just go and do it now.'

He turned his back on the surly goblin and re-joined the obsidian stone searchers.

'I'm going to look in Mr Goblin's cave,' Carran told his sister and the brownie.

'It won't be in there,' Tobrien told him. But Carran was already at the entrance of the cave. He went in, beckoning his sister to join him. Tobrien turned to help one of the dryads search under a pile of fallen leaves once they had disappeared out of his sight.

'I'll stand guard, and warn you both if he comes back,' a gnome told the humans.

When the humans eventually stepped out of the cave, all heard their voices of celebration and delight. Tobrien ran towards them, eyes wide with excitement.

'You've found it? Where was it?'

'Under the goblin's bed', Rosalie informed him triumphantly. 'We reckon he must have seen you drop it and pounced.'

'Sounds like the sort of thing he would do', the brownie agreed.

'He's coming back!' one of the dwarves yelled. Tobrien put the obsidian stone in his inside coat pocket. Everyone stood still, and waited, stony-faced for the goblin to come closer.

'What you all looking at me like that for? He asked, glowering at them. 'It's not my fault you're all wasting your sad, pathetic lives looking for something so trivial and insignificant.'

'If it was so trivial and insignificant', said the gnome who had kept watch outside the goblins' cave while the two humans had searched painstakingly inside, 'why did you keep it in your dark, miserable abode?'

The goblin turned purple, lifted his hands towards the gnome and started hissing out a black magic spell. He would teach the insolent fool a lesson!

Whatever the gnome was supposed to be turned into however, or whatever bad thing was meant to happen to him, never did. Instead, a howling zephyr, brought about by one of the sylphs came down and lifted the surprised goblin off the ground, and took him, as the sylph explained to the young human folk, to Fairyland, where the king and queen would deal with him and punish him as they saw fit.

Amid cheers from the elementals and magic wielders, Tobrien led Rosalie and Carran to the abode he shared with his wife, but not before they met up with the elven jeweller, who made the obsidian stone into a beautiful necklace.

At first Tobriens' wife looked surprised when her husband came home with two human folk, but being a good hostess, she made them feel welcome and they were all soon sitting down to a good, hearty meal. After they had all finished, she presented Tobrien with the wedding anniversary present she had made for him - a beautiful, embroidered cushion for him to kneel on whenever he needed to while working in the park. In return, he gave her the obsidian stone necklace, and that was when he explained why he had bought the college students home.

There would be tales to tell when they both got home, and always a warm welcome from Tobrien, his wife, and anyone else who had worked alongside them when they hunted for the lost obsidian stone that was to be a gift to mark a very special date.

On Adventure

*(**Poem written by Zachary Fyldon, a student at one of Fantastica's schools. It is from an English lesson, and the teacher interviewed by a journalist from the Museum of Literature stated that the class had to write a piece of poetry that described some of the things they did in real life.**)*

I travel through the sky in my father's jet, passing over snow topped mountains and watching the red sun set.

Sometimes I let myself be lifted by a kite.

Below me the crowds stand under yellow lamplight.

At the touch of a button I teleport myself to lands afar and ride in style in a flying car.

I open the portal to another dimension with a golden key and wander through mystical landscapes as far as the eye can see.

Over the bridge I travel by express train then through and over rugged terrain.

On a magic carpet I traverse exotic climes and in a machine journey back through time.

The journey to adventure never ends, and it's even better when you travel with friends.

A variant on the above poem

By *Zachary Fyldon*

I sped through the sky in my father's jet, got tangled in the Dark Lord's sky-net, and I still haven't escaped from his dungeon yet.

I was lifted and carried away by a bird, a kite.

The crowd stared in helpless dismay at this sight.

Alone they left me to put up a desperate fight.

I teleported myself to a land far away, was sold by merchants into slavery, and they cruelly tested me on my bravery.

I opened the portal to another dimension with a tiny key. It slammed shut and vanished, trapping me. I wander, afraid, through this hellish place I want to flee.

Over the rickety bridge I travelled by express train.

I was recaptured by the slave-merchants once again. They found me trying to hide behind sacks full of grain.

On a magic carpet I flew over strange climes, was nearly killed by aliens several times, and fell victim to people committing crimes.

The journey to adventure never ends, but for your own protection, travel with magic-wielding friends.

Pillow from the Sky

*(**Elaina and Gabe told their story to Cristen Queensberry, 'Mage Chronicles' journalist. They still have the gift of being able to see the little folk, unlike their parents. It is worth noting that just because someone is born and bred in Fantastica does not necessarily mean they can see the little magical folk or the ghosts**).*

Elaina and Gabe were excited. Quite understandable really, as they were going to stay for a couple of hot summery nights with their friend, Fairy Honeyberry. They were fourteen and fifteen now, respectively, and had known the tiny winged lady since they were small children. One day back, the two little ones had gone, in all childhood innocence and belief, to seek out the fairy-folk. They had come across Fairy Honeyberry sleeping in a hole in a tree in the woods, and their footsteps had apparently woken her.

Then came a series of adventures, which I won't go into, of which the grown-ups later said, smiling down at them, "Yes, children, that's a lovely story", or "My, you do have quite an imagination, don't you?" Not one of the adults ever said "Could I come and look for the magical folk with you?"

Perhaps that was a good thing. It meant that it could remain their childhood secret.

But Elaina and Gabe grew up, and their friend was forgotten for a long time. It was only when they went on a school trip at the ages of thirteen and fourteen to the local Museum of Witchcraft and Wizardry through the Ages and went into a tiny room by themselves, that they met a wise old man who told them that they had a friend who missed them. They had no idea who he was talking about.

'Fairy Honeyberry,' he said simply. 'Come with me, and I'll show you'.

'Won't they miss us?' the teenagers hesitated.

The wise man waved his right hand about as if conducting an orchestra, or casting a spell.

'Not now, they won't. Come with me'.

Elaina and Gabe followed the mysterious fellow down a passageway that twisted and turned like a rollercoaster. It continued until they reached the woods where Elaina and Gabe had first encountered Fairy Honeyberry. The old man tapped an ancient oak tree.

'Fairy Honeyberry? You there? I have visitors for you'.

'Visitors?' The miniature woman stared at Elaina and Gabe for what seemed to them to be an eternity. Then a smile spread across her face.

'At long last! Elaina! Gabe! How grown-up you are now! Please, tell me what you've been up to since we lost contact'.

Gabe explained about school, and what they did outside of it, and he apologised on his and his sister's behalf for neglecting Fairy Honeyberry's friendship.

'It happens', the wise man joined in. 'Very young children are open-minded, so they see the little folk, but as they grow up, many stop believing. I think that is what happened to you both. Now you can heal the rift in the ring of friendship between you and Fairy Honeyberry'.

I could tell you how the conversation ended, and how they got back to their fellow travellers on the school trip, but instead I shall move onto what happened when they went to stay for a couple of nights with their magical friend.

Fairy Honeyberry had put out a huge dome for the three of them, outside on plain grassland, just outside the woods, and where the stars could be seen. Blankets made from eiderdown, and embroidered by pixies would keep them warm.

'We'll need a pillow too', said Fairy Honeyberry, and standing on the highest leaf on a nearby tree, she stretched out both arms, and down into them floated a white cloud from the sky.

They fell asleep to the sound of birdsong, and dreamed about sitting on fluffy white cloud pillows while sylphs played their golden harps.

It was a beautiful night to sleep with your head on a pillow from the sky.

(*NOTE: Cloud pillows are quite abundant in Fantastica, and are sold from the smallest corner shop to the largest supermarket. Prices vary, with the smallest clouds costing the least and the biggest clouds costing the most. Choices range from pure white to sunset pink. However, please be aware that there are places where fake cloud pillows are sold, which are actually just bunches of cotton wool. The best ways to avoid these sham items is to avoid shops in the back streets of Fantastica, and those where goblins are the shopkeepers).*

Presents for My Friends Birthdays

(A friendship poem, penned by another pupil at a girls' only school in Fantastica. She actually bought a jewellery box for her friend Jessica's birthday, and tells 'The Mage Chronicles' it gave her the idea for this poem. All names mentioned are of people in her English class.)

A jewellery box for Jessica

An emerald ring for Eve

A ruby-encrusted purse for Ressika

Ultramarine crystals for U'neeve

A luxury log cabin for Lauren

A gold xylophone for Xarina

A quartz bangle for Quarren

Edelweiss for Erina

A diaphanous scarf for Delia

A velvet bathrobe for Vicki

A violet gown for Velina

A zaffre-coloured clock for Zindie

A zircon watch for Zoe

A white snow quartz for Wanda

A marble ball ornament for Melody

A dream-catcher for Dana

Rainbow Bubbles

(A poetry competition is held at Fantastica's Museum of Literature on the thirty-first of March, every year. This poem was given first prize last year by the judges and was written by Hugo Paisley, a pupil of one of Fantastica's high schools. The original poem he wrote, which had a completely different theme, was destroyed by bullies on the day that the competitors needed to hand their work to the judges, which meant he had to come up with something else fast).

Fascinated, people watch, gaping in wonder, at the black velvety sky, and at the mysterious rainbow bubbles that float above and below them

Texting on mobiles.

Shaking each other, and pointing up at the sky.

"Can you see them?"

Excited cries, sending a message that there is something exciting to be seen

These rainbow bubbles are a phenomenon, the wise elders will tell you. Could it be that an ancient god or goddess will appear?

Or does the cosmos have other ideas?

Skylights

(This year's winner for the Museum of Literature poetry competition is Aria Orlando, an undergraduate at Fantastica University. She is reading a degree in witchcraft and defence against black magic, after her non-magic-wielding parents were killed by wizards for her mother's topaz necklace that she was wearing that fateful day. Aria escaped to her grandmother's house. The poem has been written in their memory).

There above the world burns the sun, a spherical furnace, a fiery skylight over our planet.

There above the world shines the moon, a silver chandelier, a glowing skylight over our planet.

There above the world sparkle the stars, specks of silvery-white glitter, twinkling skylights over our planet.

There above the world flutter the tiny fairies, glowing little elementals, casting their sleeping spells on the people of our planet.

There above my parents watch over me, my guardian angels to guide me and keep me safe.

Somewhere Else

(This article tells the story of when a resident of Fantastica visited its neighbour, Fairyland for the first time. It is kept at Fantastica's Museum of History).

Vaienna watches as Taia roams round the history class, handing out party invitations like sweets. Aiden, who sits next to Vaienna, has got one. She steals a glance. You can see that they were created electronically and printed off in colour. Taia must have taken a lot of time over them, she thinks. As one more person gets an invite, and Taia sits back down at her desk, Vaienna's heart sinks. She never gets invited to anything anymore. It's her parents fault. Every time she is asked to come to a party or rave-up, they make excuses why she shouldn't go. Now everyone has given up asking. Her parents are too strict, they say to each other. Glad we don't have parents like that.

Mr Hazen watches as Taia wanders round the class. He couldn't care less. He'll be retiring from his teaching job soon anyway.

Someone else can come and maintain discipline, and tell them to sit down and get on with their work. His mind wanders to the cottage in the Cotswolds he is moving to with his wife. She's going to retire from her chef job. No more bratty, delinquent kids. No more pesky teenagers. In front of him, the class works on researching the ancient Greeks and Romans. At least some of them do, except the ones who doodle on paper, or consult their I-phone under their desk.

She walks home later with Taia, who firmly tells her she needs to learn to stand up for herself. Didn't her mum and dad ever go out to parties when they were young? What did they think was going to happen to their precious daughter? Taia gets home first, and Vaienna walks the rest of the way alone.

'Vaienna!'

She turns round, not recognising the voice, but noticing how beautiful it sounds, like the tinkling of bells. Behind her stands a fairy, and her pale-pink hair cascades in curls down to her tiny waist, wearing a white shimmering dress.

Vaienna can see silvery-blue butterfly wings. How lovely it would be to have wings and be able to fly, she thinks.

'I'm Persaidya. I've come to take you to the Fairyland Annual Party,' the magical being tells her.

'I've nothing to wear.'

'Haven't you?' The fairy raises her hand, and at once, Vaienna's school uniform is transformed into a satin lilac dress that reaches down to just above her feet, encrusted with tiny amethyst stones. It has a sparkly black belt that matches her shoes. Her cumbersome school bag is reduced to the size of a large purse, black and encrusted with more amethysts. Persaidya takes Vaienna by the hand, and they fly to Fairyland.

'What about my parents?'

'Don't worry. I've dealt with them. They'll welcome you home afterwards.' She says no more about it, but Vaienna suspects that magic is being used somehow. No one gets past her parents. She should know; she's their daughter.

Fairyland is the most beautiful, ethereal place Vaienna has ever been to, even though her own homeland, Fantastica, comes pretty close. She can only look round in wonder, as they land and walk towards the majestic palace of King Oberon and Queen Titania. She can see fairies, pixies, elves, salamanders, sylphs, peri, even vampires and centaurs, and she watches, as merfolk and naiads swim upstream to the palace.

'Welcome,' the regal couple say, smiling at her, and the party begins.

Everyone who attended Taia's party gossips about it in Spanish the next day, until Mrs Crofter decides enough is enough and orders them to be quiet and get on with their work, saying that they have enough time for conversation at lunch break. Vaienna discreetly checks her mobile phone under the desk. Mrs Crofter is nothing like the soon-to-be-retired history teacher. If she catches sight of a mobile phone or I-phone being used, she confiscates it.

'Tut, tut, playing with your phone in class', whispers Taia to her. They sat together.

Mrs Crofter had her back to the class, sorting out paperwork on her desk. 'Let's have a look at those pictures'.

Taia looked at the pictures that her friend had taken at the party in Fairyland.

'Wow! Those costumes are brilliant!'

'Quiet please! Concentrate on what you have to do', Mrs Crofter turns round to face Taia. 'This is a classroom. You are here to read, write, type and learn, not to sit round gossiping like old ladies in a café'.

Vaienna walks home with Taia and a few others.

'Have you seen Vaienna's pics?' asks Taia. 'I didn't even know she was going to a party. How did you manage to get your parents to let you go out?'

'Did they get their costumes and make-up done professionally?'

'This is Fantastica, remember? The nearest place to Fairyland?'

'Hang on!' one of the girls says. 'I thought it was a myth that Fairyland was that close to us. Could you get one of your new fairy friends to take us there? We'll see if this place really does exist!' She laughs, and others join in.

Vaienna summons Persaidya in the way she was taught at the party. There are astonished gasps as the fairy magically appears before them.

'Let me take you to the world of the little folk', her tinkling bell-like voice tells them, and off everyone flies, by way of magic, to a land some of the pupils in the school, Vaienna being one of them, has already been, eyes wide in wonder and amazement at the beautiful and ethereal land they find themselves in. It will be something to tell their children and grandchildren in the future.

The Aromatherapy Massage

(Holistic Enchantment is one of Fantastica's go-to places for all kinds of holistic treatments and therapies. Astra Noel is a regular visitor to Fantastica, as she works as an actress and stunt-artist here, as well as being a magical performer. Newspaper columnist, Lexi Ridlington, tells Astra's story).

Astra was twenty and in her first job, as a part-time shop assistant in a clothes store aimed at people in their teens, twenties and thirties. She had ambition, (she wanted to work in theatre or film and maybe be an actress). She was talented, had studied drama at school, and was currently studying it at college, but her parents had insisted that she stay in "proper" employment for a while, before trying to reach for her dreams of working in the performing arts industry or at least while trying to do so. Her manager at work, Eileen, was even harder to get round.

'What's wrong with working here, she would grouch. We pay you a decent wage, you're entitled to plenty of holidays, you work with nice people and we give you enough time off already, to go to college'. Eileen always moaned whenever any of her staff asked for time off. Most of them would ask the deputy manager, Zenia instead. How they longed for Eileen to either leave or retire!

She made an appointment to have a day off work, choosing a day when she didn't have to attend college, to have an aromatherapy massage, and Elaine grouched about that too.

'Couldn't you go some other time', she complained, when Astra asked for a particular day to be absent from the shop. 'This is a business. You can't just go gallivanting off when and where you feel like it. Anyway, I don't really see the point of having a massage. All you do is just lie there, and waste time.'

Astra felt a strong, horrible, sense of guilt, and confided in a colleague, Sullivan, when Eileen was out of earshot, that she might as well cancel the appointment.

'Why should you? If it was Zenia, she'd say yes straightaway. There's nothing to feel guilty about. It's not as if you take a holiday every day!'

On the day she took leave from work, she walked round to a place called Holistic Enchantment, a place she had never been into, but had walked past many times. You couldn't see inside. The windows were stained glass, like those in a church. Astra pushed open the gleaming silver door and found herself in a beautiful garden. The Zen music mingled harmoniously with the water fountains as Astra walked along a sparkling pearl coloured path. Soon she came to a black onyx reception desk in the shape of a semi-circle.

'Hi,' the girl behind the desk smiled at her brightly. 'Can I help?'

'I've got an appointment for an aromatherapy massage', Astra told her, taking in the receptionist's lilac coloured hair, and long black robe and cloak.

'Could I take your name?'

'Astra Noel'.

'Okay'. Then Astra watched in amazement, as the young receptionist moved her right hand in the air as if cleaning an invisible window, and an avatar of a fairy appeared in the ether above her.

'My next appointment has arrived?'

'Yes, Fairy Jasmine. Would you like her to wait here?'

'It's all right, Crystal-Tranquillity. I'll come through now. Astra of the humans, I take it?'

The avatar vanished and Astra watched, entranced, as an ebony-black door to her right opened, billowing out blue mist, and from this colourful mist, a fairy emerged. She took in the ethereal creature's sky-blue dress; pink, white, and blue-patterned wings and light pink hair.

The fairy radiated peace and relaxation, which made Astra feel somewhat calmer.

'Thanks Crystal-Tranquillity. Astra? Please, follow me.'

'I've never seen a fairy before. Is Crystal-Tranquillity human like me?'

Astra couldn't believe she was actually talking to one of the '"little folk"', although this fairy wasn't exactly little. She was taller than Astra.

'She's a mage, trained in the holistic arts and when not on the front desk, she gives hot stone therapy,' Fairy Jasmine told her.

'Could I learn magic?'

She imagined turning Eileen into a cockroach. Ha! She'd probably still moan then, Astra thought.

'I'll give you a card when your session is finished, and then it will be up to you whether you wish to pursue the art of magic. I advise you to think about it carefully though.

No point in wanting to have magic powers just for the sake of having magic powers. You need a purpose, a good reason, but whoever you choose to be your tutor will tell you all this'.

They made their way back through the black door, through the blue mist, and down a garden-corridor with small trees and flowers in bloom. There were more windows like the ones Astra saw before she had entered this mysterious place. They came to another black door and into the aromatherapy room. Here, there was a massage table covered with soft fluffy towels and burning candles on the shelf. Pan-pipe music played softly. Fairy Jasmine mixed the essential oils of lavender, ylang-ylang and orange as her human client looked on.

'These will help you to relax and unwind', Fairy Jasmine told her softly. Astra lay face-down and closed her eyes, as the magical being massaged her back. She could have stayed there forever, she thought. All too soon she was sitting up with a blue glass of cold water, and then she was taken back to the front desk where Crystal-Tranquillity was waiting.

'Did you enjoy it?'

'It was lovely', Astra said truthfully.

'She's interested in learning the art of magic', Fairy Jasmine told the mage. 'Could I take one of these cards to give her?'

'By all means', said Crystal-Tranquillity with a smile.

Astra left Holistic Enchantment with a sense of peace and wonder, and a card in her pocket.

What would her family, and everyone at work, say when she told them that she had spoken to a mage, had been massaged by one of the fairy-folk, and had a contact card for the School of Magic Arts?

What indeed?

How I Learnt the Art of Magic

By Astra Noel

During my visit to Holistic Enchantment, I had the privilege of being pampered by one of the fairy-folk of Fantastica. Being in the presence of a magical entity made me wonder if I too could learn magic. However, rather than say yes straightaway, my ethereal therapist, whose name was Fairy Jasmine, advised me that I should not want to learn to do magic just for the sake of it. I needed a purpose, a good reason.

So I thought long and hard. Why did I wish to learn to possess magical powers? For one thing, not many humans had it, except for the mages. In the end I chose self-defence, and having seen plenty of sorcery-wielders who carried out their craft in order to entertain and amuse others, and earn a wage while doing so, I decided I would like to do the same myself. I would escape, not from my job, which I enjoyed, but from a certain individual who had made life hard for me – Eileen, my manager.

I attended my first magic-wielding lecture with a group of other humans at Fantastica University, where I would study under the tutelage of Professor Nadir, a wizard with years of spellcasting experience under his belt. He told us what Fairy Jasmine had previously told me, and he added that we should never use magic for reasons of sinister intent, such as revenge. Used wrongly, and in a spiteful manner, sorcery was extremely dangerous. He told us what he says is a true story, about an incident he was involved in years ago, as a young trainee teacher of Witchcraft and Wizardry –

"Back in my younger days as a tutor, before I had gained enough experience that would allow me to be made a professor, I was teaching a small team of novices how to become magic-bearers. I did everything I could to make the lectures informative and inspiring to the students and they found it refreshing after the strictness of some of their other tutors. Yet there was one thing I should have done, but didn't, and that was to drive home the importance of knowing why one wanted to learn to cast spells. Would it be for self-protection? Entertainment purposes?

People who live in Fantastica know that being a magical performer is a well-paid job and always has been. Being young and impatient, I wanted to teach my students as much magic as I could. If I had known, one of my students, whose name was Josep, would have been made to leave the university. He had only wanted to study this art form as a means of vengeance against a friend who he had fallen out with.

It hadn't escaped my notice that Josep was a student of few words. I thought nothing of it. Perhaps he was shy, or preferred to speak out when he felt he had something worthwhile to say, rather than engage in idle chatter. After all, there were other students who were on the quiet side. I failed to realise that he was brooding, like a storm that is far off on the horizon, but is on its way. One day, Josep told me that he had a friend, Hillar, who was interested in learning wizardry and asked if he could join the lectures. I gave my permission, elated to have gained the interest of yet another student, and the next day Hillar came to participate in the study of witchcraft and wizardry.

The class was given the task to turn an object into something else entirely. It was a simple concept, but the actual practice wasn't so easy.

Some novices picked it up quicker than others. Hillar was one of them, turning the crystal ball on my desk into a fountain that could have graced the royal gardens of Fairyland. Three more, Lekika, Jorg, and Clara, took their turns before Josep did. When the time came for Josep to turn an object into something else, he murmured words that none of us could hear, and I politely asked him to speak louder. Then there were gasps of horror and I saw that Josep had turned Hillar into a rat.

Worse still, he had done it on purpose and you could tell by the sly smile on his face, as he made his way to the door. I stood in front of it, blocking his path, and ordered him to change Hillar back. Josep refused, so I did it myself.

I dismissed the class for the day, and brought Josep and Hillar before the University Dean, Professor Lilija Periwinkle to deal with the incident as she saw fit.

She took a dim view of it, and told Josep, quite firmly, that using magic during a heated argument, when you felt angry and vengeful, was harmful. Mercifully for him, he was allowed to stay on at the University. On the other hand, there would be no contact allowed with Hillar for three months. I saw Josep's jaw drop in dismay. Hillar looked relieved. Both boys left Professor Lilija's office separately.

Three months later, and to this day, Josep and Hillar made peace between them. A fellow teacher saw them together, and, making himself invisible, undetectable, ventured towards the boys to separate them once more. He stopped when he came close enough to hear Josep's apology to Hillar, and how he missed him. It sounded sincere, and turned out to be so.

Josep learned the dangers of using magical powers in anger, and I learned to always make sure that I knew exactly why each and every novice I taught wanted to study the art of witchcraft and wizardry."

The Cottage

(Fayah is a long-time resident of Fantastica. Her parents still work outside of the area. She is a qualified mage, having worked under the tutelage of the wizard Lord Stargazer. She shares a home with her coal-fire friend Coral and two friends, Hikaru and Vanja who are well-practiced in the art of white magic while her parents still own the cottage that once belonged to Auntie Gladys. Fayah wrote this story before she even met either Hikaru or Vanja).

'Now be good for your Auntie Gladys, Fayah, and we'll see you when we come back. Take care of her and mind you behave yourself'.

'Oh we'll be all right, won't we, dear?'

Auntie Gladys smiled sweetly down at me, but I knew the truth behind that smile. It was all pretend. It made me feel ill. As soon as my parents were out of the way, her attitude would change completely. Auntie Gladys was Mum's sister and unlike Mum, had never married. Probably just as well.

Anyway, who in their right mind would want to marry Auntie Gladys? It was a pity my parents had to go on these 'business trips' like they were now. They both worked for the same big company, outside of Fantastica. If only I could have gone with them. I watched and waved as the car got farther and farther away from Auntie Gladys' cottage, hatred and fear like lead in my stomach.

'Freda! Freda, come here!' Auntie Gladys grabbed me unceremoniously and practically hauled me into the cottage as if she had just kidnapped me off the street. The car had disappeared round the corner by then.

'Don't just stand there gawping and waving like a twit', she snapped. 'There's work to be done! Here, mop the kitchen floor!' Nasty, horrible woman. 'I'll mop you if you speak to me like that again,' I thought.

The kitchen floor looked clean enough already, as if Auntie Gladys had just done it, but I knew her well enough just to take the mop and do the floor again, though I would have loved to whack her with it.

I didn't bother telling her that my name was Fayah; she still called me Freda. Sometimes, for some reason, she'd call me Prudence, or Doris. Girls names from another era. This was the twenty-first century for heaven's sake. She did it on purpose, and I didn't even like those names.

'What are you doing?! Just wipe the darned floor, instead of gaping out of the window! You stupid, lazy, dozy little imbecile.' Then she knocked the bucket of soapy water over so I had to clear up the mess. Then she swept out of the kitchen.

She was a horrible person, and just look at the state of her. I nearly sniggered out loud at that thought and had to cover my mouth quickly before she heard me. I got more attention from her than I wanted, which didn't take much as I didn't want *any* attention from her. After a while, I crept out of the kitchen, my mopping finally done, and went to peek at what Auntie Gladys was doing. Good.

The monstrous thing was asleep in her armchair and she called *me* lazy! What a complete hypocrite. She was quite fat too. Nothing against fat people. I know quite a few overweight people.

Our next door neighbour is one such person, but she is a lovely, jolly individual, and she bakes delicious cakes and sells them to our family and other people she knows. I turned to go back in the kitchen before Auntie Gladys woke up and caught me staring at her.

'How you put up with her, Fayah, I'll never know.'

I turned round in surprise, and saw the coal fire, burning merrily in the grate, looking at me. It had a female voice. It looked like any other blaze, but there was a young girl's fiery face among the flames. I wondered whether she was a goddess of fire, like Vesta or Hestia. I didn't know what to say at first. I thought I was going loopy, like the cantankerous old hag in the living room. Just being in the same house as her would make anyone go loopy.

'How long have you been here?' I asked the first thing that came into my head.

It seemed a stupid question to ask a fire, even if it could talk, and I expected it to say that it had only just been lit a few hours ago, but instead she replied,

'I've been burning since before you first came here. I've watched you and your Auntie, and I've seen and heard how she treats you. Tell me,' the blaze continued, 'how old are you now?'

'Eleven', I said.

'You should be able to come here and have fun here and outside in the garden. Instead, your Auntie, if you can call her that, keeps you cooped up in here every time you stay and barks orders at you to fetch and carry and do her household chores, and what thanks do you get?'

'None,' I admitted, wondering where this conversation was heading.

'Yeah, you're right. You get none. Anyway, let's go in the kitchen, before the cantankerous old dragon (and apologies to dragons) wakes up and starts moaning again.' We made our way quietly as possible into the kitchen.

'What shall we do now?' I whispered. 'We can't do anything too noisy, or Auntie Gladys will hear us.'

'Tell you what we'll do, the coal fire said. 'Move that tapestry out of the way. I'd like to show you something.'

I did as I was told. I was used to doing that. Underneath the tapestry was a door. From when I was a year old until now, that same tapestry with its pictures of fruits and vegetables, had always been there, but I had never known that there was a door behind it.

'Wow,' I said, searching for something better to say. It seemed a bit lame to just say "wow".

Then we heard the armchair creaking, and we knew that Auntie Gladys was awake.

'Prudence! Go and fetch me a blanket! I'm freezing! I shouldn't have to ask you. It's winter, and obvious that people need to be warm.'

'Prudence!' The coal fire imitated my Aunties' harsh, nagging voice, and I put my hand to my mouth to stifle my giggles. I was glad she was with me. 'Fetch me a blanket! Quick! I'm turning into an icicle. I'm too bone idle to get it myself!'

Then we stopped giggling and poking fun, as we heard Auntie Gladys coming.

'Prudence! Do I have to ask you twice to do everything! Stupid, idiotic girl. All right, don't bother, just sit and skulk in the kitchen and expect me to do everything, like the nasty little creature you are.' It's not me who's nasty, I was dying to say, but self-preservation stopped me. Probably just as well.

'Quick, she's coming', the coal fire hissed, and we escaped through the door and the tapestry fell back over it.

'For heaven's sake, where is the little twit?'

We hurried through the dark stone passage, the coal fires' glow lighting the way. I was excited, but nervous too. What if she caught up with us? Eventually, we came to another door and stepped through it into a round room. There was an empty fireplace and the coal fire went straight to it. I stared round the room in surprise. I had come here all this time and never even knew this room was here!

'It is a bit like a living room', I agreed, 'with the pictures on the walls, and the corner unit with ornaments inside, and everything. It's really pretty'.

'I've come here every single night I've been burning,' said the coal fire. 'I can't trust your Auntie Gladys to leave me alone. If I burned in the fireplace with her knowing, then she'd probably put me out just before she went to bed. If she saw me wandering round the cottage, then she'd call the fire brigade.'

'You're right,' I agreed. 'Except that she'd probably be too scared to ring the fire brigade herself, and would make me ring them while she got out of the house quick. That's how mean and selfish she is.'

We both laughed. Auntie Gladys was a bully, and like other folks of that sort, she was a coward. In the face of danger, Auntie Gladys would be the first to try to get away. If she had been the leader of an army in battle, she would have led from the back, instead of the front, where the brave leaders would be.

'By the way', I suddenly thought, 'I've not asked you what your name is, or if you have one. You already know mine.'

'You're right Fayah, I do. Mine's Coral.'

'Coral? That's a nice name. There's a girl in my school called Coral'.

Just then, we heard footsteps, and Auntie Gladys's ever-dreaded voice.

'I know you're here somewhere, Maureen! It's no use trying to hide. I'll find you, and won't you be so sorry'. The threatening tone in her voice was frightening.

Auntie Gladys would never call me by my proper name, except when my parents were there. She got on my nerves.

'She's found the door underneath the kitchen tapestry,' said Coral. She saw the alarm on my face. 'Pull up that trapdoor; we'll get away from her that way'.

The door-handle of the room we were in suddenly turned as we got ourselves beneath the trapdoor.

'Maureen! Maureen!' She was shouting now. 'Grow up and stop playing your silly little game or I'll belt you, and don't think I don't mean it, because I do.' I didn't want to find out whether or not she would carry out her threat. She'd belt me? Not if I belted her first.

As she ranted, the door opened, and we pulled the trapdoor down and hurried down the steps until we came to another passageway. It was dark, and only Corals' glow lit the way. Eventually we came to another door. This one led into a beautiful garden, with trees, flowers, fountains, statues and sculptures.

'Come on,' Coral urged me. 'I know where we can go.'

We eventually came to another cottage, just as humble and innocent-looking as the one that horrible Auntie Gladys lived in. Coral ushered me inside.

'Do you come here as well?' I asked, surprised. That was two places Coral could go to keep away from my Auntie Gladys.

We entered the cottage, and were greeted by an ancient man, who had horn rimmed spectacles perched on his nose, and was wearing a silver cloak. I couldn't help staring at him, even though I knew staring wasn't a polite thing to do. Sometimes you couldn't help it.

'Greetings, Coral. You've come to keep me warm again, I see. I say, who's your young friend?'

'Meet Fayah. Fayah, this is Lord Stargazer, a wizard who has lived here for over a thousand years. He gave me the ability to do what you humans can do, such as see, hear and talk'.

Lord Stargazer? That sounded like a good name for a wizard. Lord Stargazer was very friendly, and he listened as Coral and I told him what it was like for me having to stay at Auntie Gladys' house while my parents were away on business. When we had finished, Lord Stargazer got up from his chair, and went to a cupboard. He got out what looked like a mirror, and he put it flat on a table. Everything that had gone on, we saw and heard again.

'To think that your parents do not know your Auntie Gladys as she really is! It is high time that something is done. I shall cast a spell, and she will be transported to a place where she will be a servant to a family of goblins. They will keep her very busy. But be aware. You will never see her again.'

Excitement bubbled inside me. No more Auntie Gladys! Yippee! Sorry Mum, I know she's your sister, but seriously, who wants a sister like her?

As we looked at the magical mirror, we saw Auntie Gladys come out to peg washing on the line. We could hear her too. I didn't want to hear her.

Her voice grated on me. But I endured it. I knew it would be worth it.

'That selfish little pig should be doing this for me. But no, instead I have to struggle by myself as usual. Well, when she comes back, I'll greet her with the cane'.

We knew what she meant by that, but she never got to see me again, or use her cane to hurt me, for she just suddenly vanished without a trace, obviously to be a servant for some goblins. I giggled at the thought of them telling her to mop the floor. Good riddance to Auntie Moan-a-lot.

'Go back to the cottage; your parents are on their way', Lord Stargazer told me. I stood there at first, trying to take in what had just happened, so Lord Stargazer had to give me a gentle push.

Coral and I headed back, and we waited in the living room.

My parents' car soon turned up the drive and I hurried out to meet them.

'Where's Auntie Gladys?' Mum asked me. 'She'll want to say bye'.

'She's disappeared', Coral told her. She'd come out to meet my parents too.

My parents looked at me, then at Coral in surprise. Mum stared at Coral and I had a sneaking suspicion she was going to faint. She didn't.

'Good grief,' Dad commented, hardly able to get his words out. 'What's going on? He stared at Coral in surprise. 'I must be going loopy! What's going on?'

Mum didn't seem to be able to speak. Most probably overwhelmed, I thought. Coral winked at me, and we took my parents into Auntie Gladys's living room to explain what had been going on. Mum hugged me, seemingly recovered from her astonishment at seeing a fire with a face and said she was sorry. Dad said he was sorry too. They hadn't realised what Auntie Gladys was like when they weren't in her presence. When our house was sold we moved into the cottage. We spent time re-decorating it all, as, let's put it this way, Auntie Gladys's taste in decor left much to be desired. Coral continued to live with us, and had the fireplace to burn in. We took my parents to meet Lord Stargazer, who became a valuable friend. He explained everything that had happened to me while I had been in Auntie Gladys cottage. Over time, my parents got used to Lord Stargazer and Coral, and we would all laugh when we were out and saw the look on the faces of people we met.

Looking back, I was one of the luckiest girls in the world, with kindly parents and a wizard and a young coal fire called Coral as my best friends.

I still think, or rather, know that I am.

The Waterfall Picture

(Many shops in Fantastica sell magical pictures; that is, pictures that are animate or into which a person can gain access into other realms. They are sold for a good price, and can be paid for by money or by donating a gift or two of good quality. Below are extracts from the diaries of Fantastica schoolgirls Sophie and Megan, and a local historian).

Everybody has pictures or posters on their bedroom walls, but they're just still, just silent, just *ordinary.* Like me, you can look at them and think 'that's a nice picture', or not, as the case may be. Take my friend Megan for example. Most of her pictures are ordinary, nothing to write home about, except for one.

The picture of the tiger in the field, the picture of a beach, with white sand and blue sky and a couple of tiny white clouds, the picture of a Chinese symbol meaning 'Good Fortune', surrounded by green leaves, not to mention the other pictures she has hanging up – they're so ordinary, so every-day!

No sound or animation. I much prefer pictures that move, that have life in them. My favourite of hers is 'The Waterfall Picture', because, when you switch it on, the water cascades down the rocks. I know what her bedroom looks like because I often walk round to her house so we can walk to college together.

Sometimes she comes to mine. All my pictures are my own artwork, which my IT technician dad has kindly put onto flat screens around my bedroom wall, and which become animate whenever I switch these flat screens on. Every three months or so I'll change the pictures so I have something different to look at. I also recently got a purple glitter lamp and often focus on it when I'm meditating. Yes, I'm into that sort of thing. Today is Saturday and I've got to clean and tidy my room on the orders of Mum and Dad. I'll put on some music. It won't be such a boring chore then.

The 'Waterfall Picture' was beautiful. During daylight hours it sat inert, but at night Megan would flick the little switch and the picture would light up and the waterfall would cascade down over the rocks, and the green bushes would light up. She didn't know how it came about, and no, she wasn't dreaming, but one Saturday night, after a day of tidying and cleaning her room, she lay in bed watching her waterfall picture, and the way the water was cascading over the rocks and then, before she knew it, she suddenly found herself there in the picture! She was amazed to find herself standing on rocks, with the waterfall flowing past her, so close. The green-leafed trees and bushes were real too. Megan touched them. Yes, they were definitely real, and so was the wind she felt gently brushing against her face. She climbed up the rocks, being careful as she did so, because the wetness made them slippery.

Eventually she stopped, and to Megan's delight, she saw a beautiful rainbow below, the end farthest form her going down into the depths of the cascading waterfall. Water nymphs played nearby in the water. If only Sophie were here!

The next day, Megan's mum comes into her bedroom, followed closely by me, Sophie, Megan's friend from college. The room is unusually quiet.

Usually Megan has really loud music on, and her mum will be hammering on the door, then barging in, shouting "Turn that racket down! Sophie's here!"

'Strange. Megan's not usually this quiet', Megan's' mum tells me.

'Doesn't look like she's here, Mrs Dowry', I say, probably looking as puzzled as my friend's' mum. I certainly feel it. Then we happen to look up and see Megan waving to us from the Waterfall Picture.

'Come inside', she is saying, though we can't actually hear her say anything. How do we get to her? She puts her hand out to us, and once my hand touches hers, I vanish into the picture. Megan's mum follows suit, but not before going to get Megan's dad. She doesn't want him to miss out. When we are all in the waterfall picture, we can hear each other, although we compete with the thunder of the water. We don't know how we're going to get out again yet, but first we shall explore.

The little group explored their new surroundings for a good length of time. They saw a sign that said 'Welcome to Oida – Land of Water Nymphs', quite close to where the waterfall thundered. Underneath, it stated that it was quite close to both Fantastica and Fairyland and could all visitors please refrain from dropping litter as this was an area of unspoilt beauty and the Oida council wanted to keep it that way. They walked away from the area where they had first entered the picture, and found themselves in a valley, where toadstool houses were dotted here and there. There were more waterfalls, from which rainbows could be seen, and there were ponds, rivers and streams. In every single one, more nymphs were spotted. There were trees and bushes and flowers that grew taller than Sophie, Megan, and Megan's' mum and dad combined.

There does come a time to end a certain adventure however, and they needed the help of the water-nymphs. After undertaking various challenges of varying degrees of difficulty, there was just one more task they needed to do.

It seemed really easy in comparison to some of the other challenges we had done. All we needed was to find the blue glowing cylinder, as that was the object that would return us back through the waterfall picture into Megan's bedroom, back in Fantastica. The streams, ponds and rivers were all a beautiful blue colour, which made finding a blue cylinder all the more difficult. We searched in waterfalls, and those of us who were agile enough scaled the trees. We looked everywhere, or thought we did, but to no avail.

'We need to think outside the box', Megan's dad told us, after most of us were exhausted and ready to give up. Perhaps it had been a bad idea to come here. But he wasn't one to give up so easily, and he wouldn't let us, either.

In the end, the cylinder turned out to be in a water-garden right beside one of the toadstool houses, except it wasn't a cylinder, but a series of pieces like a jigsaw puzzle. Once Megan (as she volunteered) had completed it, a blue cylinder, ten centimetres long, glowed in her hand.

Immediately, the magical object began to pull Megan along, and the rest of us took hold of each other's hand and allowed it to tug us back to where we had first entered the waterfall picture.

Megan kept the blue glow-cylinder in her bedroom, to serve as a nightlight and a guide, and she and Sophie talked about their adventure during a sleepover at Sophie's house the following night.

Through the Air

(Folk-song written by a witch, based on words actually spoken to young children training in witchcraft in eighth century Fantastica. Unfortunately, there was a protest against witches and their spellcasting in the twelfth century, and they went into hiding until the uprising was over and it was safe to practice and teach witchcraft. Nowadays, this song is as popular in Fantastica as it was the first time, and is sometimes performed during a dance and song ceremony. It is also sung as a lullaby, and there are more verses).

Follow me, children, with the cool wind brushing our faces, as we ride upon our broomsticks

Follow me, children, as we sail under the wispy clouds, and over our Mother Earth.

Follow me, children, to the immense crystal cave, where we shall have tonight's magic lesson.

Tour

(St Imogen of the Druid Priestesses is one of Fantastica's top schools, and is also one of the largest. Below is a recording, used for educational purposes, of a former student of the school and teacher-in-training giving a tour of St Imogen's to a group of potential future students and their parents. It gives an insight into what a typical school in Fantastica is like).

Welcome to St Imogen of the Druid Priestesses School. My name is Kimberleigh, and I have been coming here since I was four. I am now eighteen, and am staying on to train here as an Art and Design and English tutor.

According to ancient legend, a chief Druid priestess called Imogen had the idea of setting up a school to train novice druids in the local area, and since then, both Druids and people of other various religions and beliefs have come here to learn together. Anyway, I shall now take you on a tour of the school. Please come with me…

This travellator we're on now takes us to the Art Cube…and this is it. It's made of reinforced glass. The computers are used for graphic design and those capsule shapes you can see are our pods. They hold everything we need for each lesson. We often play varying genres of music to help bring out the creativity in the students. Now we'll move on this way…

We have our biology laboratory here. Each glass cube you see holds everything to do with this subject, be it human, animal, or plant biology.

Next door you can see what we call "The Fusion". This is where the pupils do their chemistry lessons. The room is specially designed for the experiments that are done under the supervision of the teacher. Then, if you follow me…

This is the 'Legacy of Shakespeare Theatre'. This ancient theatre has undergone many revamps and refurbishments in its time, and it has a futuristic theme these days.

Modern and futuristic technology is used for special effects in performances. Actors can even float in the air or shoot lightning from their fingers.

I'm now going to take you all outside now and to the 'English Home'. Each floor is themed, from the ground floor to the fourth. You can also see the 'English Country Garden' which is used on nice days…and here, just next door, is 'The International Station', where students are educated in Spanish, French, and Italian during their first five years here. After that, they can choose as many as five extra languages. They have mini restaurants, shops, hotel receptions, and so on, to help assist the pupils in learning the languages fluently. Furthermore, the teachers themselves are from the native countries of the languages being taught…

Back here in the main body of St Imogen's, we have here the Geo Dome, where geography is taught. Wall screens and special effects technology are used to teach the students about weather, volcanoes, maps, and anything that is to do with this subject.

If you follow me, I'm going to take you to 'The Relic', where history lessons take place. You can see that this is set out like a theatre/cinema. The lessons are quite interactive and you can watch as well as join in with the past life of our ancestors.

Then, if you come with me, we'll visit the 'Pythagoras Area', where everything to do with maths is taught and this is it. Directly opposite, you can see what is known as the 'Isaac Newton Electro-Cube', where physics is taught.

We'll go down this travellator now, and here we'll get off and walk on the normal floor to 'Faith Suite'. It's all along this corridor and each room is a mini church, synagogue, temple, mosque, and any other holy place that believers of different religions go to worship their god or goddess and so on.

Just two more places to show you all.

Here we have the Textiles and Technology Warehouse, and you can see the machines used for creating things from wood, metal, and plastic, as well as the computer or IT section.

Electronics is also used here. Then lastly, if you'd like to follow me…

We have 'The Druid Suite'. This is the oldest and most sacred part of the school. The only other part that is sacred is our religious studies corridor known as 'Faith Suite', which we visited earlier. The bronze plaque you can see here in the stone floor is dedicated to the school's founder, St Imogen of the Druid Priestesses. This is where pupils learn everything about Druidism…

Well, thanks for coming everybody. I'll guide you back to the Grand Entrance which is attached to 'The Druid Suite', and I hope to see you and your children if and when they start here in September.

Travelling on the Bus

*(**A documentary written by Seanna Branning, a first-time visitor to Fantastica who is employed as a magazine journalist all over the world. She travelled with a group of Fantastica residents on one of their buses. Here is her report below).***

We are waiting for the bus. A man is looking at his watch. *Please let the bus come soon. It's boring waiting ages for public transport.* People are having conversations. They are all going to do their shopping, or to meet up with friends, except one girl, Nicki, who is on her way to a job interview. The elderly woman she is speaking to wishes her luck. Nicki wants this job, believing it to be ideal for her. *Ah, here's the bus now. No, you get on first. You got to this bus stop before me.*

It's the number seven bus, going to a town called Eldwiq. That's where everyone is going, except for the few that want to get off en-route.

As soon as the last passenger from the bus stop steps on and pays the driver, the bus moves on as he finds a seat and sits down next to a woman with a large handbag. Everyone on the bus has been to Eldwiq before. Some of them go there regularly, and they know the route the bus takes.

We're going through a long tunnel. Since when did this bus go through a long tunnel, someone asks. There is a little one, where the road dips down and then back up, but that goes under a railway bridge, and isn't much of a tunnel, so I am told. This one goes on for ages, and is made of glass. You can see the plants and flowers growing on the outside. Pots with roses, gerberas, hyacinths, and many other flowers adorn the inside edges of the tunnel.

The bus comes out the other end, where there is usually a garden centre. No garden centre now. It's a forest with deer, squirrels, weasels, and birds. *Oh look?! There's a badger. I love badgers!* There are people too, but tribal folk, with painted bodies, and hand-held spears, wearing jewellery they have made themselves, and straw skirts, regardless of their gender.

They stare at the bus in astonishment and fear as if it is a terrible beast, and their instinct is to chase after it, following it with their war cries and their hurled spears, until the bus has left them far behind. The spears do no damage to the bus, but the people inside are unnerved. Those tribal folk seemed rather dangerous, and hostile. Then we all come out of the forest, and the bus stops outside a little cottage. We're all told to get off, and follow the driver. What's going on? Nicki is on her way to interview! How on earth is she going to get there on time? What about the people who want to do shopping and meet up with friends?

We are all in the cottage now, having been welcomed in by a little old woman, Wanda and her granddaughter, Niamh. No ordinary cottage, this. Everyone is ushered into the living room, and offered a cushion to sit on. As soon as people sit down on a cushion, it slowly and gently rises, so not only is everyone sitting on a cushion, instead of a chair, they are sitting in mid-air. There's a log fire too, but this one isn't burning in a fireplace on or against the wall, it is right in the middle of the deep-purple carpet, contained by the silver bowl. Drinks all round.

This is elderberry cordial. What are you drinking? I've got some lemon and jasmine tea.
There are animated pictures on the walls. There's one of a great cruise ship, actually sailing. *Look! You can see people moving about on deck.* There's a picture of a thatched-roof cottage with a pretty garden. The people in this picture are actually doing some gardening. There's a picture, also, of children playing in the park. The girl is actually going back and forth on the swing, and the two boys are going up and down on the see-saw. Such unusual pictures, and did you notice something else? There was sound. There is also a broad wooden ledge, a mantelpiece that goes round all four walls. There are candles burning, their flames unusually huge and orange. There are ornaments too, and crystals and gemstones. There is no wallpaper on these walls. There are just paintings of different-coloured flowers, and it is a surprise to find that these don't just look like real flowers, they smell like them, too, and they keep changing colour. *Did you see that? This yellow flower has just turned red.*

We are all invited to have a look at the dining room. *Wow, look at this!* Big forest, with picnic tables dotted here and there.

There's even a children's playground, with slide, see-saw, helter-skelters, swings, roundabouts and a climbing frame. There are statues dotted around here too. A man is aiming an arrow at the sky. A woman is in a ballet position. A girl is doing a cartwheel, and a boy is flying an aeroplane. All of them, stuck in one position.

Then there is the kitchen. State-of-the-art, like the ones you see on those cooking programmes. The sort you wish you could have.

Three bedrooms – one is for Wanda, the other is for Niamh, and the third is a guest room. They have visitors sometimes, you know. The bedroom for the old woman is a beautiful garden, with trees and flowers, and bushes. There's even a vegetable patch, and am I right in thinking that's a little herb garden just there? I thought so. The hammock is in between two oak trees. Niamh's' room looks like outer space. There is a metal capsule thing, floating vertically, and that's what she gets into at night. The whole room is dark, but there are stars and planets whizzing by on the walls, and shooting stars. You float in this room.

The guest room looks pretty interesting too. Perhaps 'exciting' would be a better word. It's a castle, with slits for windows like in the real medieval castles, and there is a four-poster bed with a canopy, and there are portraits of important-looking people. Outside, you can see a moat, and a drawbridge below you. What a lovely house. We all thank Wanda and Niamh for their hospitality.

That's fine. Do please come again, they tell us.

I leave this unusual house, ready and eager to explore whatever else this mystical land of Fantastica has in store for me.

Tunnel

(There are many strange and magical tunnels in Fantastica. This particular one is known to locals as the "Randomation Tunnel". The poem below was written by two friends and is kept in Fantastica Museum. As a word of advice, get as much information on tunnels you wish to enter. Trust your instincts. Not all tunnels are harmless – some have been known to make people disappear without trace, others harbour undesirable and dangerous entities. Your best bet is check with the Fantastica Information Centre and to travel with an experienced guide).

Through the tunnel we walk.

The curved ceiling twinkling with starry lights makes you feel as if you're under the night sky

The silver brick walls have windows. You can see beautiful landscapes that look like an artist's fantasy paintings.

As we walk further through the tunnel, the starry lights and silver bricks have gone and the fantasy landscape windows too.

Through the rest of the tunnel we walk in total darkness except for the neon bar-lights that reach from floor to wall to ceiling.

We love walking home through this tunnel, and it fascinates us how it always looks different, every time we travel along here.

Vinegar Bottle

(Recorded by a gnome who was witness to the conversation between a wizard and a young woman, Amy-Cindra, who had been sent to him for training due to being spotted by talent scouts for her 'abilities'. She originally resided in Peterborough, England, but was treated with suspicion and hostility. The final straw came one night, when a large, aggressive, group of people surrounded her cottage, shouting abusively, crying out for "the witch to be burnt at the stake, like her ancestors before her". She managed to reach the passageway under the cottage just before some of the baying mob managed to force their way into her abode. Amy-Cindra was forced to leave her hometown with nothing but the clothes she stood up in, and start afresh in Fantastica. Many people who have been shunned or persecuted in their own towns, cities, or countries, due to their magical or psychic abilities, come to live in Fantastica as it is seen as the norm to possess these kind of powers).

Come, my friend, look inside this malt vinegar bottle and tell me what you see.

I see a stretch of deep amber sand stretching on for miles. Above, the sunset is so vivid and so red. I perceive a bright-red sea, and the river that trickles down to meet it. The sun is reflected in it.

You see me turn the vinegar bottle. This time I notice that thin trickles of luminous bright-red show beneath the deep-red-brown liquid. This, I can see from here, is lava from a volcano, and the red-yellow 'sparks' are fire-entities going about their work in the forges inside the hot lava.

This time, looking at the malt vinegar bottle from *this* angle, I see a red river and reddish-brown rocks. I can also perceive the sun's glowing reflection, and I'm pretty sure I can see an image of one of the merfolk.

See? Those who are ignorant and unobservant will only see a brownish-reddish liquid. You see so much more.

You have the gift.

Willow Tree

(Willow trees are as common in Fantastica as anywhere else. However, there is one that has caught the attention of visitors to the place. Below are newspaper quotes from people around the world who encountered the phenomenal willow tree in Fantastica. Not everyone believes them. There are plenty of sceptics abound, who feel that the folk that have spoken out about seeing unusual events concerning this particular willow tree are either drunk or deluded. Indeed, the strangest thing about this drooping plant is that nothing that happens ever shows up on a photograph, only the tree itself, so it is very difficult to prove that you have seen anything out of the ordinary, even if you are accompanied by witnesses).

'"I had visited Fantastica with a friend of mine. On our way back to the portal that would take us back to our home country, Brazil, we passed the willow and we saw a couple sitting on a rug drinking from a flask, and laughing and chatting under the drooping branches. However, their clothes looked as if they were from a by-gone era. As we drew closer, they slowly faded away'" - Javier, 25, Brazil

"I was just taking my dog for his last walk, as I always do in the evening, in Fantastica, as I live quite close to one of the portals that allows outsiders access to it. We noticed that there were lights twinkling. They were blue, white, and even silver. I'd never known anyone to put lights on this tree before so I went to have a closer look. It turned out that it was the fairy-folk" - Amalia, 45, Romania

"I was on my way home from the city where I work, when I saw a door set inside an elm tree. Intrigued, I ventured forth into the mysterious land called Fantastica.

 I passed by a willow tree and noticed that there was a fire burning there, on the grass beneath the drooping branches. Around it were people dressed in what I would describe as biblical clothes, the sort of clothes that people like Moses and other people in the Bible would have worn. As I came closer to them, the people disappeared," – Matthias, 19, England

"My wife and I work in Fantastica, while an au-pair looks after our seven year old daughter back home in Tonga. Not so long ago, we (my wife and I), drove past the famous willow tree and noticed what appeared to be blobs of colour. Upon getting out of the car and going for a closer look, we saw that these blobs were actually flowers," – Eloni, 38, Tonga

"I live in a house with a garden that has a trapdoor leading to Fantastica.

One night, I saw rocks beneath the willow tree and sat upon them, was a beautiful mermaid. She vanished as I approached her" - Ganizani, 59, Sudan

"A friend of mine and I were staying in one of Fantastica's five-star hotels. We were taking a walk one evening before heading back. On passing a certain willow tree, we saw tiny creatures among the drooping leaves. My friend believes they were either tree-fairies or earth elementals, called dryads" – Divina, 20, Philippines

"I work at a car garage in Fantastica and I was walking back to the trapdoor that would lead me back to my own country when I passed a willow tree. I saw that there were steps on the grass under the branches. Being the curious person I am, I ventured down them, to find to my surprise, a landscape with hills, mountains, fields and deserts stretching as far as the eye could see" – Han, 30, Switzerland

"As I passed by the willow tree that I have heard so many people talk about, a door appeared, almost hidden by the drooping branches. Curious, I ventured towards it, and found steps leading up to a room filled with artefacts and ancient relics. Some of them seemed to be imbued with what I thought was magic" – Ambre, 46, France

"There was a table under the willow tree when I got near, which wasn't anything out of the ordinary in itself, but there were familiar objects on it in warped shapes – a doll-sized bed, a fork, a lamp and a candle. Then the table floated upwards and away, carrying the mysterious objects with it"– Aleksandar, 20, Bulgaria

"Until recently, I would have laughed if anyone had told me I would be able to fly without wings, yet, when I passed close to this willow tree that stands proud in Fantastica, I found that I could do exactly that and I floated among the branches.

I have made several visits to this magical country ever since" – Eirian, 30, Wales

"The famous willow tree that I have heard so many stories about was surrounded by wispy, colour-changing mist when I passed by it. There was music that was the most hauntingly-beautiful I had ever heard" – Kalju, 47, Estonia

Why not see the willow tree for yourself?

Yoga Class

(*This is a recording of a typical relaxation session done at the end of yoga classes in Fantastica, and can be experienced at Fantastica's yogic hotels. Please feel free to use the meditation below for your own yogic class or personal use*).

Welcome to today's yoga class. We'll start by sitting on our mats in the lotus or crossed-legged position. Place your hands palms upwards, resting on your knees.

Breathe slowly, and as you inhale, feel yourself getting calm and relaxed, and as you exhale, feel the tensions of the day dissipate into nothingness. Breathe and feel that you are becoming more and more relaxed.

As your mind relaxes into a tranquil state, slowly levitate into mid-air, and float peacefully for a moment. Gently come out of this position and curl into a ball. Softly backward somersault and stretch out your legs ready to touch the floor as you land.

On your yoga mat, go into mountain pose. Slowly bend into crescent moon pose…then back into mountain pose. Next, position yourself so you are now in dancer pose…then slowly glide into half-moon.

Next, bring yourself back into mountain pose…then chair pose. Bring your arms down by your side, and gently levitate again into mid-air. Bend into dancer pose…then warrior pose…now half-moon. Then softly, slowly, bring yourself into tree pose and allow yourself to float down to your yoga mat.

We shall now go into the five pointed star pose…then glide into prayer twist. Take yourself into pyramid position, then bend into downward dog. Stay with this for a moment...then bring yourself into tree pose…then mountain pose…then bring yourself down into tiptoe position.

Presently, we come to the relaxation part of our yoga practice. Come into lotus position…….float once again into the air, around half-way between your mat and the ceiling, and uncurl into dead mans' pose or 'shavasana'.

The lights are dimmed down and you can see the stars. Close your eyes and float among them and while the music softly plays, be aware of your inhale…and…exhale…

When you are ready, come once more into lotus position and float back down to your yoga mat. In your mind, be aware of how relaxed you feel.

Now the lights are slowly brightening. Gently wriggle your fingers and toes. Bring your palms together and bow your head.

Thank yourself for the strength, peace and tranquillity you have experienced in today's yoga class and I shall see you again next week.

Namaste.

Milton Keynes UK
Ingram Content Group UK Ltd.
UKHW020959140124
435997UK00008BA/28

9 781634 905237